GRIFFIN'S CASTLE

Also by JENNY NIMMO

THE CHILDREN OF THE RED KING SERIES

Midnight for Charlie Bone
Charlie Bone and the Time Twister
Charlie Bone and the Invisible Boy
Charlie Bone and the Castle of Mirrors
Charlie Bone and the Hidden King
Charlie Bone and the Beast

THE MAGICIAN TRILOGY

The Snow Spider
Emlyn's Moon
The Chestnut Soldier

GRIFFIN'S CASTLE

JENNY NIMMO

SCHOLASTIC INC.

New York   Toronto   London   Auckland   Sydney
Mexico City   New Delhi   Hong Kong   Buenos Aires

THIS BOOK IS DEDICATED TO
THE MEMORY OF THE LATE RAY SMITH.

ISBN-13: 978-0-545-11708-1
ISBN-10: 0-545-11708-9

12 11 10 9 8 7 6 5 4 3 2 1   8 9 10 11 12 13/0
Printed in the U.S.A.   40

First Scholastic paperback printing, December 2008
Book design by Alison Klapthor

Animals do not sleep. At night
They stand over the World like a stone wall.

The Face of a Horse
Nicolai Alekseevich Zabolotsky
Translated from the Russian by Daniel Weissbort

AUTHOR'S NOTE

All of the characters and some of the locations in this book are fictitious. But there is a many-towered castle in Cardiff and a famous animal wall, where fifteen carved stone creatures watch and wait.

CONTENTS

A Broken Griffin

A tall house loomed before Dinah. She stood at the gate, trying to make out what it really looked like, but its features were blurred in the gloom. So she had to rely on her imagination and saw narrow lancet windows and the great oak door of a castle.

On either side of the wild lawn, trees swept from the wall to the house. They stood in rows, dense evergreens that whispered and covered the garden with shadows. Once a wide path had led from the gate, but weeds had cracked the paving stones and a tide of silky moss lapped at the neat edging. Dinah approached the house by hopping onto the clear patches of stone, telling herself she would drown if she trod on the moss.

Dinah's mother, Rosalie, unlocked the front door. A moment later light swept into the garden, but the house remained faceless and mysterious, still a castle. And now, above the roof, moonlight silvered a bank of clouds, turning them into snowcapped mountains.

"Come on, love." Her mother's tired voice drifted down to her.

But Dinah stood enthralled. Ever since she could remember, they had wandered between rented or borrowed rooms, sometimes staying for a month with Auntie June or Gran. Once Dinah had lost her mother altogether and been taken into foster care. But now they had a house, a castle of their own. She began to mount the five worn steps up to the front door and noticed a row of rusty palings that half concealed a basement window. Jumping from the steps to investigate this hidden room, Dinah felt her foot strike something hard that seemed to split in two. She picked up the head of a bird, and when she retrieved the second piece of stone, she found that the two halves made a small griffin, an eagle's head and wings with the body and hindquarters of a lion.

"Griffin's Castle," Dinah murmured.

"What are you going on about, Di?" her mother called impatiently. "Shut the door when you come in. It'll take hours to warm this place."

"I'm home," cried Dinah, carrying the broken griffin inside. The word *forever* ached to be said, but Dinah dared not use it yet.

She dropped her two backpacks in the hall. One held her clothes; the other, a bright patchwork affair, contained her treasures. She put the broken griffin beside them. She would find a way to mend it, she promised, patting the rough feathers on its head.

The ceilings were high, and there were no carpets. Their footsteps echoed up the damp stairwell as they climbed to the first-floor landing. Rosalie dumped her suitcase against the wall and looked about her, rather forlornly, before moving into a large room at the back of the house.

"I hope they remember to bring a heater," she said, observing the stained wallpaper and dusty floorboards.

The room looked grim in the harsh light of the bare overhead bulb. But Dinah, half closing her eyes, saw a four-poster bed curtained in rich brocade and a rose-colored carpet sweeping up to the long window.

"It's obvious where the queen will sleep," she said.

"Oh, be quiet, Di!" Rosalie sighed.

Dinah retreated to the landing and eyed the narrow staircase that beckoned to secret attic rooms.

Rosalie came and sat on her suitcase, cradling her chin in her hands. "Gomer said he'd be here," she said, "with beds and stuff all ready for us."

"And a welcome with open arms," added Dinah. But when her mother glanced up reproachfully, she felt guilty and said, "Traffic's bad. I bet he'll be here in a sec."

Dinah had never met Gomer Gwynne, although he was Rosalie's employer, friend, and savior. She had imagined someone tall, whose armor glinted. Someone with dazzling eyes, possibly blue; a toothpaste-ad smile; and a horse of unbelievable whiteness. Even when she replaced this image with something more realistic, the eyes and teeth remained, and to these she added a dark suit and glossy brown hair. For Rosalie deserved the best; she was beautiful, and soon, perhaps, Gomer Gwynne would be Rosalie's husband and Dinah's father.

Her true father, Billy Jones, had gone down to the docks and skipped aboard a freighter when Dinah was three months old. He was young, and so was Rosalie. They had never seen each other again. But Rosalie kept his photograph in a silver frame and set it up where her Dinah could see it, in their damp studio apartments and rented rooms. And Dinah had grown up with this image of a teenage boy with curls and a crooked smile. A face she'd been told to love but did not, nor could she bring herself to tell Rosalie that the grinning boy meant nothing to her. She dreamed of someone strong who wouldn't run away from his responsibilities.

And Gomer Gwynne had turned up. So Dinah had

pinned her hopes on the man who, so far, had provided them with a roof and might soon bring food and furniture.

Gomer Gwynne owned three restaurants. He was rich, he was generous, and he was going to take care of them, Rosalie said. He had already turned Rosalie from a waitress into a receptionist, with the extra wages this brought.

Outside a van hooted, and Rosalie sped downstairs. Dinah followed hesitantly and clung to the newel post while she closed her eyes and prayed that Gomer Gwynne would be the gallant knight they needed.

"Di, where are you?" called Rosalie.

Dinah drew back, her eyes still closed. Footsteps hammered on the oak floor, and she smelled cigars and spicy aftershave. Her eyes flew open and met the steely gray gaze of a tall, lean man with silver-black hair and a mustache. He was not the man they wanted. Dinah couldn't hide her disappointment.

Gomer held out his hand and said, "Well, Dinah?"

She could tell that he was not very pleased to meet her. Rosalie had evidently failed to describe her daughter accurately. Perhaps Gomer had expected a cute little girl, not someone almost as tall as her mother, with a sallow complexion and dark hair that refused to curl. It had happened before. People assumed she would look like Rosalie. They seldom managed to hide their surprise or disappointment. "Where'd you find her, Rosie?" someone once joked. Dinah was only five at the time, but she never forgot it. As she took Gomer's large, cold hand, Dinah could feel the life she'd hoped for slipping away. She would have to fight for her castle.

He glanced at her backpacks and the broken statue. "What have you got there, girl? No animals allowed." It was meant as a joke, of course, but Dinah didn't laugh.

"It's a griffin," she said gravely. "I found it in the garden."

Gomer raised an eyebrow and extended a foot.

Dinah noted the expensive leather shoe as panic gripped her. But he didn't touch her patchwork bag. He merely said, "And what's in here?"

Climbing the stairs, Rosalie called gaily, "It's paper, Gomer. Pictures and stuff from old magazines. She's a funny girl, aren't you, Di?"

Dinah snatched up her backpack, feeling betrayed.

A young man called from the front door, "Shall we bring the gear in now, Mr. Gwynne?"

"Right away, boys," Gomer shouted heartily. "Mrs. Jones will show you where it's all to go." You could tell he was used to authority.

"I ought to clean the place first," Rosalie cried from the first-floor landing. "It's so dusty."

"The girl will do it, won't you, Dinah? Here comes a broom." And from a closet in the hall he produced a broom, a dustpan, and a brush. With a smile that had no warmth in it, he held them out to Dinah.

Dinah laid her treasures close to the staircase and took the broom.

"Start with your mother's room," Gomer ordered. "Rosalie, come down and have a drink."

Rosalie gave Dinah a wink and squeezed her hand as they passed on the stairs. "Cheer up, love," she whispered. "It's going to be all right."

Dinah was not convinced. As dust flew around her in the queen's bedroom, the old despair began to weigh her down, and the empty room, which, a moment before, had been full of promise, seemed just as desolate as all the other hopeless places she'd shared with Rosalie.

"I'm not part of his plan," she murmured. "What's going to happen to me?"

She knelt and brushed her pile of dirt and peeled wallpaper into the dustpan, picturing the grand four-poster bed again. And now she clothed it with lace-edged linen and a satin quilt. And lying on the quilt, a queen with golden hair who smiled in her sleep.

We could make this a fine home, just like it once must have been, Dinah told herself.

Was this a home?

She laid the dustpan, brush, and broom against the landing wall and traced the sound of laughter to a kitchen. Rosalie, Gomer, and two young men were drinking wine and dipping their fingers into bowls of nuts. The room seemed crammed with furniture after the echoey places upstairs. Fitted cupboards lined the walls. There was a sink, a hutch, and, around the table, several pine chairs.

"Di, come and celebrate," cried Rosalie, whose face was flushed and shiny. "You are a love. Come here."

Dinah moved into the room, and her mother clutched and hugged her. "This is my Dinah," she told the young men. "She is my best friend."

"Hi, Di!" said the young men, raising their glasses. One was very thin with a bad case of acne and the beginning of a mustache. The other was big-boned and freckled and more than made up for his friend's skinny frame.

"Where are we going to put your bed, then, Dinah?" Gomer asked.

"Under the roof," she said. "At the very top."

"But, Di, won't you feel lonely up there?" Rosalie asked anxiously.

"Of course not," Dinah said grimly. "I'm eleven."

"Come on, lads! Al, Bob, get moving!" Gomer said.

The young men almost sprang to attention. They emptied their glasses and ran out of the house, like soldiers under orders.

Dinah looked hard at Gomer while he poured another glass for Rosalie. *He could pass for a knight,* she concluded, *though one getting past his prime.* The mustache fit and the abundant silvery hair. *If only he wasn't so frosty.*

"Whose house is this?" she asked.

"Mine," he said gravely.

"But you don't live in it."

"Dinah," Rosalie warned, "don't push."

"It's too large," said Gomer. "I have an apartment on the waterfront. My mother used to live here, but now she's . . . elsewhere." And because Dinah continued to stare at him, he admitted, "She's in a home for the elderly."

"Can I visit her?" Dinah asked.

A look almost of horror passed across Gomer's face. "Why?" he demanded.

"I'd like to. Old people know things. They keep pictures. They remember the war."

"Is that so?" he said, standing up.

"Well, can I?" Dinah demanded.

Gomer turned away and walked out the door. "No," he said. "She wanders. Visits confuse her."

Rosalie ran after Gomer, saying, "I'm sorry, Gomer. She's just excited. She isn't usually like this."

I am like this, Dinah thought. *I'll always want to know things.*

The young men were carrying furniture upstairs. Dinah followed them. They stopped on the second landing, and Freckle-face said, "Are you sure you want to go up there?" inclining his head toward the shadowy third staircase.

"Yes," said Dinah. "Into the attic."

There were two attic rooms. Both had cracked, sharply sloping ceilings and faded blue wallpaper. Dinah chose the room with a long dormer window overlooking the trees. Al and Bob could hardly see what they were doing until Rosalie came up with a bedside lamp.

"It's so lonely up here," Rosalie said. Dinah thought, *She's scared of being alone, two floors down, but I'm happy to be free.*

Gomer furnished their new home in a very temporary fashion. There was nothing for a sitting room. Most of the furniture was for Rosalie's bedroom: a large bed, a white dressing table, and a mixed collection of wardrobes. She even had an armchair and a television. Dinah was left with a bed, a table, and a chair.

"There's nowhere for my clothes," she complained.

Gomer ignored this, and Rosalie seemed reluctant to mention it. "You can share my closets," she whispered. "And I'll give you my radio now that I've got a T.V."

It was after midnight when Gomer and his helpers drove away. Rosalie and Dinah smiled at each other across the kitchen table.

"What do you think of Gomer?" asked Rosalie, obviously confident of Dinah's approval.

"He's a bit old," hedged Dinah.

"Forty-seven's not old." Rosalie yawned and stretched luxuriously. "All these rooms for only twenty pounds a week. We've really landed on our feet this time."

"And we'll stay on our feet," said Dinah fiercely. "No one's going to push us out ever."

"I don't know about *ever*, love." Rosalie was too weary to notice Dinah's passionate expression.

"Not ever," Dinah repeated softly. She got up and kissed her mother good night. "I'm going to bed."

But not to sleep. Dinah had work to do. Up in her chilly attic, she untied her patchwork bag and held it upside down. Paper floated across the floorboards: pictures of animals, inventions, flowers, planets, and people. Poetry, stories, reports of discoveries, and descriptions of foreign cities all rustled silkily while Dinah, sitting cross-legged in their midst, began to arrange them.

When she had made several neat piles, she took a tube of glue from her backpack and, standing on her bed, began to paste the cuttings over the scars and cracks in the ceiling. She had to move the bed five times before she could cover every inch of the damaged plaster. And then she began on the walls. When her work was finished, she spread the remaining cuttings over her bed. And a lioness slipped from inside the folded picture of a castle.

Dinah seized the lioness and gazed at her. She was a golden creature; her great paws were splashed with silver as her beautiful muscled body curved above the shallow water of a stream. She might have been a

kitten enjoying a game if it were not for the deadly pur-
pose in her eyes and the fleeing wildebeest before her.

Dinah propped the picture against her lamp, and
when she climbed into bed at last, there came into her
mind an image of the same fierce lioness, prowling
beneath the evergreens outside her window.

This is my home now, she thought, *because I live
here. And I will have an animal. It will be strong and
fearless, and if anyone tries to take my home away, it
will tear them to bits.*

A cat, sheltering beneath the dark trees, looked up
at Dinah's window and called out hopefully. But the
voice Dinah heard in her dream was deeper and infi-
nitely more savage.

THE LIONESS

Gomer gave Rosalie a week off so that she could settle in and find her daughter a new school.

Rosalie spent all of her savings, including the child-support money, on curtains and dishes. And then she remembered that Dinah might need a uniform. "We'll have to find a school that doesn't insist on you looking smart," she said with a giggle, trying to turn bad management into a joke.

Dinah had found a school a mile away. "I'll have to go to Elias Comprehensive," she said solemnly. "It's the nearest. They wear maroon blazers and gray skirts or trousers."

"Oh!" Rosalie marveled at Dinah's efficiency. They were having what Rosalie had hoped would be a leisurely breakfast. The kitchen was at the back of the house, and although it overlooked a dump covered in brambles, the sun reached through the window, making the room warm and bright, unlike the rooms facing west, where the gloomy evergreens shut out the sky.

"I think you had better get me registered soon," Dinah went on. "I've already missed six weeks, and Social Services will be after you. But I'm not going until I've got the uniform. It's bad enough starting a new school halfway through the semester."

Dinah's mother often wondered if a changeling had sneaked into her baby's cradle. Dinah was not like any relative she knew. Both Rosalie and her sister, June, would have skipped school whenever possible; they had hated homework, while Dinah relished it. They had looked for the latest fashion, while Dinah seemed to prefer clothes that made her look anonymous. Rosalie hoped that her daughter was not some kind of genius; she didn't think she could cope with that. And whose genes were responsible for Dinah's dark complexion and tall, bony frame? The grandfather with a mysterious name whom Rosalie remembered stooping over her like a dark hawk when she was very small?

Rosalie sighed. "We'd better go to this Elias place today, then," she said without enthusiasm.

Dinah dressed carefully. She wanted to make a good impression. She was terrified the principal would not admit her. *How can I tell him he won't regret taking me?* she wondered desperately. Rosalie had thrown Dinah's old schoolbooks away when they moved from their chilly studio in Swansea. "We've got to travel light, Di," Rosalie had said.

"But I can carry them," Dinah implored.

"It's them or this." Rosalie had pointed to Dinah's patchwork bag and its treasured contents. And Dinah's schoolbooks, packed neatly into a shopping bag, had dropped to the floor like a stone.

"You know I can't leave those," Dinah cried bitterly, clutching her bag of cuttings.

And the exercise books, filled with perfect spelling,

faultless diagrams, and immaculate punctuation, had been torn and burned in the rusty grate. All except Dinah's history notebook, which she had managed to hide among her precious poems and pictures.

They had made an appointment for four o'clock, when the school was emptying. Dinah eyed the confident maroon-clad children hurrying home, and she plucked at the hem of her shabby parka.

The principal, Mr. Williams, was an imposing figure, the sort a principal should be, very tall with prematurely white hair. His smiles were brief and courteous and his eyes, beneath black eyebrows, rather fierce. So, before her mother could ask the wrong questions, Dinah thrust the hidden history notebook in front of him, flicking the pages quickly so that he could see the check marks and congratulations, the neat writing and absence of mistakes.

Mr. Williams was surprised. He looked more carefully at the waiflike girl clutching her chair as though she were trying to keep a grip on her very existence.

"Dinah's a year ahead," Rosalie explained. "They took her in the junior high when she was ten, so she's used to the work."

"She'll be with her own age group for the present," Mr. Williams said firmly. "We'll see you on Monday, then, Dinah."

"But I haven't got a uniform," Dinah told him anxiously.

"We won't lock you out for that." He waved a hand.

"But —"

Rosalie broke in quickly. "We'll get the clothes tomorrow. Come on, Di."

Mr. Williams returned the history book to Dinah and gave them both a longer version of his smile.

"That's settled then," Rosalie said as they walked down quiet, tree-lined Anglesey Road. "But I'll have to call Gomer and find out if he can give me next week's wages in advance."

"To pay for my uniform?" asked Dinah.

"Don't look so worried, love," Rosalie said. "I know

he'll give it to me." She popped into the next phone booth they saw. Gomer hadn't had a telephone connected in the house.

When Rosalie sidled out of the phone booth, she looked pleased but guilty. "He'll give me the money, but there's a snag. He wants me to work nights."

"Every night?" asked Dinah, thinking of the dark house and the tall, impenetrable trees.

"Seems like it," Rosalie confessed. "But there's a young couple moving into the basement. You'll be all right."

"What young couple?" Dinah was suspicious. She sensed that Rosalie and Gomer were trying to fool her.

"I don't know, love. Come on, we've got to get a bus to the center of town. He says he'll meet me at the Angel."

"Why? Why there?"

"It's where he meets people."

"But if it's a bar, they won't let me in," said Dinah, growing more desperate.

"Look, you want this uniform, don't you?" Rosalie cried, and, catching hold of Dinah's hand, she dragged her, half running, half stumbling, to the bus stop.

They had to wait twenty minutes before the bus arrived. It began to drizzle as they climbed aboard. Dinah was staring grimly at the slanting mist when something electrifying emerged through the murky twilight: the high gray wall of a castle.

"Why didn't you tell me about that?" Dinah breathed, pressing her finger against the window.

"I forgot," said Rosalie, tense and fluttery. "Come on, we get off here."

Dinah stepped out of the bus in a trance. As they followed the curve of the castle wall, she didn't take her eyes off it for one moment. They crossed the road and stopped at the entrance to an arcade.

"You'd better wait here, out of the rain," Rosalie said. "You can look at the shops, but don't wander off, will you? The Angel's just at the end of the road." She ran through the rain and disappeared around a corner.

Dinah retreated into the arcade. She stared at her reflection in a window crammed with velvet skirts and jewelry.

What a mess, she told herself. *No wonder Gomer's trying to shake you off. He is, you know.* She nodded at herself.

A boy, passing behind, looked over her shoulder and said, "Cheer up!"

"I heard that!" She wheeled around in time to see a tall, skinny boy with straw-colored hair step behind a pile of Chinese baskets.

Thunder growled behind the traffic. Dinah felt battered by the noise and the weather. How long would she have to wait? She walked out into the downpour and found the entrance to the Angel Hotel. Through tall glass doors, she saw a wide staircase leading to a foyer. Here there were glossy potted plants and crimson carpets all lit by a sparkling chandelier. More stairs, plants, and a second chandelier could be glimpsed beyond the foyer. Where were Rosalie and Gomer? Intimidated by the shiny opulence, Dinah stepped away from the glass doors and stood beneath the solid hotel awning for a moment. From here she had a perfect view of the castle. It was a pale gold color with several towers; the nearest to Dinah was a tall clock tower with a blue-and-gold clock face on all four walls, each one flanked by strange figures dressed in pale blue, white, and red.

Dinah stared at the clock tower for a long time, trying to make out the colorful figures between the clock faces. And then she became aware of the low wall that separated the castle from the road. It was crawling with animals. Stone animals.

She began to walk back to the arcade, counting the animals on the other side of the road. They could not have lived so close to one another had they been alive. There were two apes, a pelican, a vulture, a seal, a wolf, a hyena, a creature that could have been a beaver. . . .

But perhaps they were only sleeping. At night their spirits would guard the castle, and no one could get past them.

From the end of the wall, a lioness gazed at Dinah. The lioness seemed to be resting on the roof-shaped apex. Her two forepaws were planted on the sloping side of the wall; her hindquarters were out of sight. She stared, disdainfully, over the muddle of traffic and wet, scurrying people. Dinah moved closer, trying to find the focus of that long unblinking golden stare. As she drew near, the lioness seemed to move. Her gray stone coat began to glow, her eyes shone, and she turned her head a little.

When Dinah stood immediately opposite the lioness, the world fell silent.

"Come on, then," Dinah whispered.

And the lioness leaped! She flew over the busy, damp, rolling vehicles and the men and women frowning through the rain. And no one saw her but Dinah.

The girl stood motionless, her mouth still open in

her secret call. And she heard the splash of heavy paws on the wet pavement beside her. Dinah couldn't look at the empty place on the wall that the lioness must surely have left. Her limbs froze, and her pulse seemed to stop. She thought that she could not really be alive. Rain tumbled onto her bare head and slid down her neck, drenching her. But she was only aware of the warm breath of an animal on her cold hand and heard only the low rumbling purr of the lioness.

She did not need to see the creature. It was there, very close, dangerous and savage. It was closer to Dinah than any other living thing.

"Di, are you crazy? You're soaking."

They stood looking at her, Rosalie flushed and anxious, Gomer suspicious. They didn't notice the lioness in her shadow. Dinah turned her head away. She must hold tight to this new companion, or the lioness would be swept away on the heavy tide of traffic.

"The car's round back," she heard Gomer say.

The lioness grumbled softly.

"Come on, Dinah." Rosalie gave her a shove. "What's gotten into you? You'll get Gomer's car in a mess. You'd better sit on my coat."

"I can't," breathed Dinah.

"Can't what? Di, are you ill?" She couldn't see the lioness.

"No, I might lose . . ." She was being tugged away.

"What have you lost? Get a move on, Dinah."

Dinah looked back. "Follow!" she commanded in a harsh whisper.

She was whisked into a sleek black car. The doors slammed, and Gomer drove out into the road with a roar. Dinah knelt on the backseat and peered through the window. Sheets of rain slanted across headlights, flew from the pavement, and danced on car roofs and hoods in a bright haze.

The car stopped at the lights, hugged in a sea of traffic. Dinah searched the darkness on either side of the road. Nothing. The lioness had lost her. She gave an involuntary moan, and Rosalie said, "Oh, Di, you haven't gone and got a cold? Why d'you play silly tricks like that? Catching your death."

"She was teaching us a lesson, Rosie," Gomer said. "Paying us back for leaving her outside. Well, you'll have to get used to it, girl. Your mom needs a bit of space. You can't hang on to her coattails forever."

"I never," Dinah blazed. "I didn't notice the rain. I was looking at the castle. I like castles and history and stuff like that, if you want to know."

"If you say so." He wasn't going to let her get away with anything.

Dinah fought for words. She scowled at Gomer's back and caught him staring at her in the rearview mirror. The battle had begun in earnest.

By the time they stopped again, the rain had dried to a trickle and the traffic had dispersed. Dinah watched someone under a purple umbrella unlatch a gate and stride up to a white front door. She saw a cat running beside a dripping hedge and saw it stop very suddenly, its ears flattened, shocked by something on the other side of the road.

It was the lioness!

She was pacing along a high wall, her head twisted toward the cat, her body a summery gold. And Dinah almost gave a shriek of joy. The cat had seen the lioness. So she *was* there. Cunningly and secretly, she had followed Dinah home.

Gomer parked outside the gate, then led them up the vanishing path to the house. The evergreens were heavy with rain, one swollen branch drooping down onto the weeds.

Dinah listened for the lioness and heard soft footfalls in the damp, dead grass.

"Only a couple of months, Rosie," Gomer said as he unlocked the door for them. "Then I'll have you out of here, and they can come and knock it down."

Dinah, stunned by this news, stood immobile on the bottom step. "Not this house," she murmured.

"Come on, Di, you'd better get changed, right now. I'll put the kettle on." Rosalie pulled her inside. "Bring your wet clothes down, and we'll dry them over the stove."

Dinah, in a panic, put out her hand. And felt something softer than a moth brushing her sleeve. The lioness was still close.

The door closed between them.

She ran up the three flights of stairs to her room and pushed open the narrow sash window. The dank earth smells that swam up to her held a trace of an exotic and dangerous scent. The space between the house and the soft glow in the road lay like a mysterious black void. For all Dinah could see, it might have been a jungle. She changed and took her wet clothes down to the kitchen.

Her mother and Gomer stopped talking when they saw her. Gomer stood up and put on his black coat.

"All's well, then," he said, giving Dinah a false sort of smile.

Rosalie saw him to the front door, and Dinah followed. She wanted to know what the lioness would do.

Gomer turned up his collar and began to cross the garden. Dinah held her breath, but he looked careless and ordinary, and she thought, *Perhaps, after all, there's nothing there.* And then, quite suddenly, Gomer flung out his right arm and increased his pace.

Had he felt her savage breath? Did he hear her stealthy tread or smell the wild, utterly unfamiliar scent of her? He reached the gate and whirled through, closing it fast behind him.

" 'Night, Gomer!" Rosalie called.

Gomer stared at her across the untamed garden. He looked as though he had passed through a minefield.

"You all right?" Rosalie asked, too anxiously.

He lifted his hand and said coldly, "See you tomorrow!"

Dinah was triumphant. She couldn't help giving a little skip into the kitchen. She wondered if the lioness could keep Gomer out. Would he brave the invisible beast behind their gate again?

Her mother seemed subdued. For supper, she put a plate of half-cooked french fries in front of Dinah and plonked an overfried egg on top of them.

"Aren't you having any?" Dinah asked.

Rosalie shook her head. "I had a snack with Gomer," she said. "I'm sorry we kept you waiting, Di. I'm sorry for all of this . . . mess."

"But everything's great. We've got Griffin's Castle, and soon we'll buy more furniture, won't we? And perhaps I can get a paper route, and you won't have to work nights." Her voice sounded high and desperate, but she had to keep talking to stop Rosalie from saying something that she didn't want to hear. She had to tell the house it had a future and erase Gomer's treacherous words about knocking it down. But she couldn't change the familiar gritty look that Rosalie wore when she had bad news to deliver.

But all Rosalie said was, "Maybe."

"Maybe?" Dinah had forgotten how many questions she had asked.

And then her mother changed the subject completely and said, "Your great-grandmother's buried near here. I just remembered the name of the church today. St. Joseph's."

"Who?" said Dinah.

"Your great-grandmother. Gran's mother. She died when she was twenty-five. Isn't that sad?"

"What was her name?" asked Dinah, who had never thought of Gran having a mother.

"Can't remember. Olive? No, Olwen, that was it. Olwen Gwalchmai. It's written in a book somewhere at Gran's. Gran was only five when her mother died, and a neighbor had to look after her. That's why she left home so young. She couldn't stay up there in the mountains with only sheep for company. Her father, that's your great-grandfather, was out on the land all day. So she packed her bags and came south when she was sixteen. Her mother's folks lived here, but they both passed on a couple of years after she arrived."

Was that supposed to explain Gran's hostility? Her funny flare-ups and the hard red hand that smacked Dinah with such relish?

"What about him?" Dinah asked. "My great-grand-father?" She was feeling the hurt of an old man abandoned by his only child.

But Rosalie could only see her mother's point of view. "He could barely speak English," she said. "He was a farmer, and his name was Gwalchmai." As if that said everything.

"It's a beautiful name," murmured Dinah. "I wouldn't run away from a name like that."

"Don't be daft, Di. Gran didn't run away from her name."

Dinah took her plate to the sink. "Gran's good at abandoning people," she muttered. The dangerous words slipped out before she could stop them.

Her mother swung round and stared at her. Dinah wished she hadn't been so careless. She didn't want another endless chat about why Gran didn't want them. "I'm going to bed," she said, rinsing her plate and stacking it neatly.

Rosalie let her daughter go without another word. But as Dinah climbed the stairs, she could still see the anxious frown and the stiff clenched hands in her mother's lap. *Someone has to take care of Mom,* Dinah thought. *But I wish it didn't have to be Gomer Gwynne.*

When Dinah reached her room, she didn't turn on the light but walked straight over to the window and flung it open. She looked toward the city, searching for a spire that might mark the graveyard of Olwen Gwalchmai, the dead great-grandmother who had suddenly entered Dinah's life. Why had she been buried here, in the city, instead of in the mountains where she lived?

The city hummed and glittered, a world away from

the timeless hollow beneath Dinah, where a lioness roamed her territory.

"There's so much they don't tell you," Dinah said to the unseen creature, and as she began to close the window, the lioness paced out of a shadow and looked up at Dinah with dazzling eyes. The outline of her powerful body burned the darkness.

BARRY IN SEARCH
OF A SECRET

Winter held back while Dinah and her mother settled into Griffin's Castle. And Dinah began to bring the house to life again. Every day, after school, she walked through the empty rooms, telling them how fine they were. She told them their names, how the curtains framed their empty windows, the color of the carpets at their feet, and the subjects in the paintings on their walls. She even mentioned an occupant, someone small and still quite shadowy, who played in a corner and sang in Welsh.

Dinah's favorite room was on the first floor, overlooking the garden and its rows of evergreens. She called it the Harp Room because a sheet of music had slipped from behind the heavy paneled shutters when she'd tried to move them. At the top of the page some-one had penciled the words *For the Harp*.

One night someone moved into the basement. Rosalie was still at work, and Dinah should have been asleep, but she often read a library book until midnight. She couldn't see anything from her window, but she heard footsteps and a distant shuffling. The next morning she listened at the locked door in the hall that led to the basement. But everything was quiet. She wanted to ask Rosalie if her baby-sitters had arrived, but her mother always slept late and Dinah didn't want to wake her.

Dinah enjoyed her walk to school, down the avenue of sycamores. Each one was laced with silvery cob-webs, like Christmas decorations. And Anglesey Road seemed like the secret passage to a lost world, with its tall trees and wild, neglected gardens.

Behind her in class sat Jacob Rose, the boy who had surprised her in Castle Arcade. He grinned sheepishly when he saw her. Dinah noticed that he never asked questions or answered them. His reading was hesitant and ragged, and in the playground, she had seen boys laughing at him and making faces behind his back. Jacob would lash out with his fists, his face a furious dark pink.

There was another boy, small and dark, with round wire-framed glasses, who always seemed to be watching Dinah. Once she gave the boy the worst scowl she could muster, but afterward, when she saw him standing alone by the school wall, he looked so utterly forlorn, she felt sorry for the look she'd given him and found herself walking over.

His name was Barry Hughes, and his father taught history in a school on the other side of town. His mother had been a teacher, too, but now she worked part-time so that her boys would have home cooking and clean soccer socks every day. Barry's brothers were both great soccer players. Kevin, the eldest, was already into rugby, but Barry had never developed the right muscles for sports. His chest ached all winter, and he was smaller than his younger brother, Josh.

Dinah learned all of this in the fifteen minutes they took to walk around the playground together. She was good at finding out about other people's families. Perhaps it was because she was truly interested.

What Barry didn't tell her was that he had always been top in every subject, until Dinah came. This had worried him at first, and he began to hate Dinah for taking his place away. He dreamed that something would happen to her, that she'd have to go to the hospital or be called back to wherever it was she came from, that one day she just wouldn't come to school and everyone would forget she had ever existed. But after Dinah talked to him, he found it impossible to feel this way again.

At home Barry found himself telling his mother about Dinah Jones. "She gets everything right," he said, "all the time. There's nothing she doesn't know. And everyone's a bit afraid of her because she's got this look, like she wouldn't be afraid of anything, anything at all. She talked to me today for a long time."

"So where does she live, this paragon?" asked Kevin, who'd been eavesdropping.

"I don't know." Barry realized that Dinah was still a mystery. He felt aggrieved that she'd learned so much about him without giving anything away. And he resolved to put this right the next day.

He didn't realize how difficult it would be.

In English class, they were asked to invent a legend and to fill three pages if they could. Barry had an idea in his head, but he couldn't put it down. He kept gazing at Dinah's writing. Words that he had hardly heard of streamed across her page, as though they had been formed by some knowledgeable angel. She was writing about a griffin, a castle, and a hoard of gold. Barry knew that Dinah's legend would be a miracle. He felt that it was no use for him to write anything at all. The idea that had seemed so good was useless.

When he gave his work in, Mrs. Price glanced at his

half-filled sheet and then up at him. "What's the matter, Barry?" she asked.

He flushed and said, "I couldn't think of anything."

"I don't believe that. Sit down." Her voice was cold and disappointed. But he couldn't explain that Dinah Jones had made his idea seem trivial and unexciting, that he'd been hunting in his head for the sort of words she used but couldn't find any.

Barry stayed indoors at recess, pleading a headache. He watched Dinah through the window. She was surrounded by a group of girls, all asking questions, all hoping a crumb of that magical knowledge would come their way. But Dinah had nothing to tell them. She walked off with a book and, when she was alone, kept opening it, scanning a page, then holding it against her skirt while she gazed at the sky.

She's learning something, Barry thought. *She can't be a minute without cramming information into her brain.* And it occurred to him that Dinah was scared to be without the books she clung to. And he was glad to know there was something that she might be afraid of.

After school he should have gone in the opposite direction. But he followed Dinah, discreetly. He stopped, occasionally, to tie a shoelace or look into his bag. She marched straight ahead, never looking around. She turned down Anglesey Road, a street Barry had glanced into but never bothered to explore. The houses were older than those on Elias Road, older than any other houses in the area, in fact. They were set farther back from the road and looked unsafe somehow, with their loose tiles, crumbling chimneys, and cracked, moss-covered steps. Some of them had been boarded up. And although a little of their former glory lingered, an air of desolation had begun to creep about them. *Due for demolition*, Barry thought.

The road seemed empty, except for the straight-backed girl walking under the yellowing leaves of the sycamore trees. Barry had to be more cautious now. He kept close to the walls and looked down weedy pathways, his hand on a rusty gate or piece of fencing so that if she caught him, he could say he was looking for a friend.

Ahead of him, Dinah reached a gate and turned through it. Barry ran and came to a crumbling stone wall just in time to see a door close in the strangest house of all. Though it wasn't the house so much as the garden that was odd. Rows of fir and cypress trees pressed about it with a sinister sort of determination. Everywhere else, golden leaves were falling, letting in the autumn sky, but this garden was cold, dark, and mysterious. Barry could almost picture wild beasts lurking behind the dense, heavy branches. Hanging on the gate was a rough wooden sign with the words GRIFFIN'S CASTLE printed on it in thick black ink.

A light came on in a room right at the top of the house. And then a figure appeared in the window. The girl looked across at him, and Barry couldn't move.

He waited, feeling stupid, until Dinah Jones came down, opened the front door, and walked up to him.

"What do you want?" she asked.

"I was looking for a friend," Barry said lamely. "I think he lives near here."

"I've never seen anyone from school on this road." She regarded him with such intensity that Barry felt even more nervous.

"Oh," he said weakly.

Above him dead leaves swirled from the branches in a light, dry wind, but the garden where Dinah stood seemed to have another climate. Heavy and still.

"Do you want to come in?" she asked, taking him by surprise.

He was late already, and his mother would worry. But perhaps the secret of all Dinah's knowledge lay in the strange house behind her.

"All right," he said.

She led him through the shadowy garden, and Barry found he couldn't reach the house fast enough. The tall trees hardly stirred, and yet an ominous whisper issued from them.

"Is your mom home?" he asked as she closed the front door behind him.

"She should be, but she isn't. I don't know where she is. She doesn't start work till five." If she hadn't looked so resigned, Barry would have said she was anxious.

"She works nights, then," he said.

Dinah nodded. "It's not so unusual." She showed him into an untidy kitchen.

"No," said Barry. "Nurses work at night. Jacob's mom does, so he stays with his aunt sometimes. Not that I know him very well. I guess your dad keeps you company."

"I haven't got a dad."

Barry felt as though he'd dug a hole for himself that wouldn't be easy to climb out of.

"D'you want some tea, then?" She began to fill a kettle.

"Orange soda, please, or Coke. I don't like tea."

"Too bad," said Dinah. "There isn't anything else."

Barry felt exhausted. He sank into a chair, unable to sustain the effort of this difficult conversation.

"The people downstairs baby-sit me." Dinah pulled a packet of cookies from a cupboard. "That's to say they're there if I need them. But I don't."

Barry took a cookie without asking. He chewed on it, trying to look thoughtful.

"D'you want to see the rest of the house?" she asked. "While the kettle's boiling?"

"Okay." He supposed he was going to have to drink tea after all.

He followed Dinah around the uncarpeted house. Every room she showed him rang with a desolate emptiness, but Dinah did not seem aware of it. She described the rooms as she would like them to have been: curtained in brocade, carpeted in rich Persian colors, and furnished with gleaming mahogany tables and cabinets. Her tone was so confident that Barry gradually managed to fill the deserted rooms with phantom chairs and tables and to furnish the neglected house as it once might have been. He even saw the great golden harp and heard the vibrations as someone ran their fingers across the long strings. *Dinah's a bit of a witch,* he thought.

"At Christmas we'll have a tree right there." She nodded at the window in the long room that overlooked the garden. "And we'll cover it with candles as white as frost, the kind they used to have long ago. And there'll be a big fire in the grate and a basket of chestnuts to roast. And I'll wash all of the crystals on the chandelier and make it sparkle again."

Barry gazed up at the huge chandelier hanging right above him.

"And it will snow, of course," he said, plunging into the festivities she'd conjured up.

"Of course." Her smile, when it came, changed her into a girl who wanted to be as normal as everyone else.

At the end of the first landing, a huge mirror loomed like an archway. It was cracked down the center, moldy in patches, and at the apex of the stained gilt frame, a small creature, about the size of a toad, peered down at its reflection.

"It's a griffin," Dinah said. "I found another one outside, made of stone. That's why I call the house Griffin's Castle."

"Ah," said Barry, thinking of the griffin in her legend.

"D'you want to see my room?" Dinah asked him suddenly. "It's right at the top and not as grand as the rest."

"Yes," he said eagerly, for now he might learn how she managed to be so extraordinary.

It was certainly an unusual room. Walls, floor, and ceiling had been plastered with newspaper cuttings, with illustrations, photographs, and columns of figures. Dinah Jones had created a sort of cave of knowledge.

Barry stood on the threshold, lost for words. Did all this stuff seep into her while she slept?

"Don't tread on the poems, please!" Dinah said.

When she stepped between her poems, did she bend down and pluck out a word or two, Barry wondered, like you might pick a poppy in a field?

He trod gingerly between the patterns of print, then sprang onto the bed, tucking his feet under him, out of harm's way.

"What d'you think?" asked Dinah.

"Wild," he said. "Amazing. It must have taken ages."

"I haven't finished the floor."

"No? Where'd you get all this stuff?"

"Newsstands are good," she said. "And cafés. D'you know, just about every newspaper has a magazine at least once a week? People just chuck them away. Sometimes I get them out of trash cans."

"Yuck!" Barry said.

"No. They're okay. Sometimes they're wet or crumpled, but I iron them."

"Huh!" Barry looked at the floor. From the foot of the bed, a stone creature looked up at him. It had an eagle's head and the body of a lion. A griffin.

"You were writing about that," he said, pointing at the little statue.

"The griffin?"

"Yes. What's the story, then?"

Dinah sat beside him. She clasped her hands and said, "Well, if you really want to know, the griffin lives in a castle. As you can see, she has the head and wings of an eagle, but she can't fly. You could say she was disabled."

"Are you sure griffins can't fly?" Barry interrupted.

"This one can't. She guards a treasure. It's everything to her, this treasure, but people are always trying to steal it. She can't stay awake all night, so she gets the animals to help her. She trusts them because they never sleep at night. They're always watching."

The room had taken on a shadowy and enchanted look. The faces, words, and creatures on the walls seemed to stir and rustle, and Barry began to wonder if their stories were seeping into him. Would he soon know as much as Dinah? He couldn't tell if she was going to say any more about the griffin. It didn't seem as though she'd reached a proper ending.

"What happens at the end?" he asked.

"I didn't finish it."

"You did. I know you did," he said accusingly.

"I did not." She leaped up, glaring at him. "You have to wait for an ending. It doesn't just come like that. It depends on the writer's circumstances. Today I came to the conclusion that the griffin flew away. Tomorrow I might find out that she didn't."

Barry thought, *Something horrible has happened to Dinah. But she hasn't tried to banish the memory. She's just put it aside so she can keep an eye on it.*

"I'm going to repair my griffin and put her on the wall outside. Then we'll see if she can fly, won't we?" Dinah said.

Downstairs a car door slammed, and mysteries were temporarily forgotten.

"Mom's back," Dinah said.

"Heck, mine's probably in a state," Barry said, taking care not to swing his feet onto some treasured words. "I'm never late."

Dinah followed him downstairs. His hand was on the front door when it flew open and a tall man stood over him. He had a cold, handsome face and curling iron-gray hair. "Who the heck are you?" he said testily.

"Barry!" said Barry, flying past the man and a pretty woman who stood behind him.

As he slammed the gate, he stumbled over a cat lying close to the wall. It was a battle-scarred creature that looked as though it hadn't had a meal for days.

"Poor thing." Barry bent and touched the cat gently between the ears. It had a surprisingly full-bodied purr, and in spite of his desire to leave Anglesey Road, Barry found himself squatting on the ground and stroking the cat.

When he stood up, the cat rose with him and followed.

"You're in for it," said Kevin as Barry walked up the front path. Kevin was cleaning his soccer cleats on the step.

Barry ignored him. He went straight through to the kitchen and made up a story before his mother could question him.

"Sorry I'm late. I had to go home with Dinah Jones. We're sharing a book, and she left it at home." Barry pulled a novel out of his bag with a flourish. "She gave me some tea, but I couldn't phone you because she didn't have one, a telephone, I mean." He said this with confidence because nowhere in Griffin's Castle had he seen a telephone.

"So you don't want your tea, then?" said Mrs. Hughes.

"Oh, I wouldn't say that!" Barry dropped his bag by the door and sat down to fish sticks and french fries.

Outside, Kevin threw his boot at the cat who had followed Barry home. Kevin wasn't actually scared of cats, but there was something creepy about this one, with its scarred face and intense green-gold eyes.

THE BEAR

Dinah sat staring at the space between Rosalie and Gomer. She didn't want to look at either of them. Why shouldn't she have a friend in the house? Rosalie had never minded before. She had always been keen to entertain in the small mildewy dumps they had inhabited. Now they had a home to be proud of, and no one must come inside because Gomer said so.

"Why?" Dinah asked again.

"The reasons need not concern you," Gomer said.

"Reasons, reasons, reasons!" muttered Dinah. She glared at Rosalie. "Shouldn't you be at work?"

Rosalie opened her mouth, but Gomer wouldn't let her answer. "Don't be insolent," he said. "You shouldn't speak to your mother like that. She's working late tonight. Not that it's any of your business."

Rosalie said quickly, "You won't be alone, Di. The Maliks are here. Down in the basement."

"I know," said Dinah. "I heard them arrive."

"I think you should come and meet them, before . . ."

"It's not necessary!" Dinah glared at them and left the room, slamming the door behind her.

"Dinah, please don't . . ." she heard her mother call, but Rosalie didn't follow her.

Moments later she heard someone running a bath. While he waited for Rosalie, Gomer puttered about, whistling, as if he owned the place. And then Dinah remembered that he did.

From her window she watched them leave the house. Rosalie wore a new coat, and the hem of her green sequined skirt showed beneath it. She wasn't going to work.

"Liars," Dinah murmured.

She sat on her high trundle bed and drew out her pile of cuttings, but she couldn't give them her full attention. Gomer's voice kept intruding. *Not that it's any of your business!* And Rosalie hadn't said a word to defend her.

"It is my business," Dinah muttered. "She's my mom."

The light was fading, but when she pushed the switch on her bedside lamp, nothing happened. She tried the main light. Nothing.

The landing was dark. Dinah made her way downstairs. She could hear a baby crying, and the past came creeping back. She sat down quickly on the last step and pressed her hands against her ears, trying to blot it out. It was the crying and the darkness together that did it. She saw again the cold, cluttered room filled with screams.

They had been sharing an apartment with Rosalie's friend Jane, in Newport. Dinah was four, and she could only remember the room they had slept in. There had been a bed that filled the narrow space, with a high window behind it. The bed was covered with blankets, but no matter how you pulled them around you, the wind and the rain reached you through the broken panes of the loose, rattly window.

Jane was married with a very tiny baby. One night, when Rosalie was out, Jane came in and left the baby on the bed beside Dinah. The baby was just a screaming bundle, and Dinah was alone with it. She lay beside the bundle and curled her arm around its head. She was so cold, but the baby's face was burning. It seemed to cry forever, the sound tearing out of the tiny body in a kind of fury. And then it stopped, and even though the wind was wailing through the window, it sounded like nothing. The baby's silence roared at Dinah.

Later, Rosalie had come in with Jane. Jane snatched up the baby and ran out of the room. Rosalie sat beside Dinah in the dark and hugged her. "I'm sorry! I'm sorry!" she kept saying. "I couldn't get back."

Outside the room a man's voice said, "Better get him to the doctor." But the woman yelled, "What's the use?" And she had howled at the man, using words that Dinah knew were the worst she could find.

The front door slammed, and the walls shook with the impact. Jane's rage turned into the quiet moan of someone whose heart was breaking.

Then Dinah knew that the baby had died, right beside her in the dark, and she was angry with the whole world for letting it happen.

They had gone to Gran's that night, Rosalie flinging clothes into a bag like a madwoman, before dragging Dinah out into the wind. Gran lived on the other side of the town, and it seemed that they had walked all night. Dinah could still feel the freezing air biting at her face and fingers. Someone must have taken pity on them because the next thing she remembered was arriving at Gran's door in a car.

Rosalie had rung the bell, and Gran appeared in her nightgown. "Oh, God," she said. "I knew this would happen." Dinah would always remember Gran's sour face above the frilled neckline of her nightie.

She and Rosalie had never talked about that night, but it had always been there, smoldering between them like an unexploded bomb. Now there was another baby crying in the dark. And this time Dinah was old enough to do something.

She felt her way into the kitchen and found some matches. Gomer and Rosalie had been eating by candlelight a few nights before, so she knew there must be candles somewhere. She found them in a drawer, lit one, and set it on a saucer. The keys hung from a hook on the dresser, each one labeled with the name of the room it belonged to. The basement key was black and heavy. It looked as though it hadn't been used for years.

Dinah carried her candle across the hall and unlocked the door to the basement. It swung inward with a groan. She peered down into the dark well of a dusty, wooden staircase. And then a door opened beside the bottom stair, and a woman blinked up into the candlelight. She was holding a beautiful baby, dark with huge bright eyes and a mass of black hair. It stopped crying and flapped its hand at Dinah.

"What's her name?" Dinah asked, for it had to be a girl.

"Maryam," said the woman. "I can't warm her milk. The electricity is off. No oven."

"He probably hasn't paid the bill," Dinah said grimly. "Mr. Gwynne."

The baby began to cry again, and through her sobs, the woman said wryly, "I think I'm supposed to be looking after you. My name is Tahira Malik."

"I'm Dinah." Dinah stepped down into a gloomy passage. Condensation shone on the peeling walls, and the damp was so oppressive it made her breathless. The woman led her into a room that smelled of dishcloths and kerosene. There was a narrow bed against the wall and, on the other side of the room, a sink unit and a useless stove. The baby's bottle, full of milk, lay on a table, dripping. Dinah set it upright. "Won't she drink it cold?" she asked.

The woman sank onto the bed and held her baby

closer. "Perhaps." She sighed. She seemed exhausted. "But I want to give her something hot to eat."

Dinah became aware of a small boy huddled into the cushions behind the woman. She couldn't tell if he was asleep or just lying there, motionless, too afraid of the dark to make a sound.

Tahira said, "My husband Karim's firm has sent him to Edinburgh for a few weeks. He couldn't find a place for all of us, and the rents here are so expensive. And then we heard of this place. It seemed so reasonable. Mr. Gwynne promised to put in a new stove and better heating, but nothing works properly."

"I'm going to get help," said Dinah. "It's all Gomer's fault. He's got to do something. Here, you keep the candle."

"You know where he is?" the woman asked.

"I've got a pretty good idea. Anyway, I'll find him somehow."

Still clasping her baby, the woman followed Dinah

into the passage. "I feel that it's wrong. You shouldn't be out alone."

"I'll be okay, Tahira!"

The woman held up the candle to light Dinah's way, but she was shaking, and the light hovered over the wooden steps like the lamp of a ship at sea.

"Thank you," she called as Dinah stepped into the hall.

Dinah looked back. "She won't die, will she?" she said.

"No." The woman shook her head and then said more desperately, "No. No! *No!*"

Dinah crossed the hall and left the house by the front door. The streetlamps killed any light left in the sky, and the evergreens covered the garden with their tall shadows. But beyond the wall, a bright mist swirled. She had almost reached the gate when a movement in the trees alerted her.

The lioness stepped out and walked toward Dinah.

Her head was lowered, and her incredible eyes shone up into the girl's face. The creature had come to the garden every night, but Dinah had never been close to her since their first meeting, when the lioness had followed her home.

She put out her hand, but the lioness's gaze did not waver. Still, she stared into Dinah's eyes. The contact was mesmerizing.

Dinah said, "Keep them safe. I'm going to get help."

The lioness purred.

Dinah smiled and whisked herself through the gate. Before she began to run, she saw the golden creature lope toward the house. She would protect them while Dinah brought help.

Dinah ran very fast, her head up, looking ahead. A cat shot between her feet before she had time to see it. She crashed onto the wet pavement and lay there, stunned, looking at it, crouched into a dark mound.

"Stupid beast," hissed Dinah.

It was an ugly thing, so different from the beautiful

cat in the garden. This pathetic creature was torn and ragged; one ear drooped, and its coat was dull and patchy.

Dinah got to her feet. Her jeans were muddy, her hands stung, and one leg felt bruised all over. "How could you?" she demanded. "You slowed me down, but you don't care, do you?"

The cat grunted miserably, curled its feet beneath its body, and looked away from Dinah. It suddenly occurred to her that she might have hurt the animal, but she couldn't feel sorry.

"You'd better move," she advised. "Or someone will do you in altogether!" And she hurried on in a hobbling sort of run, the fastest way she could manage.

In twenty minutes she had reached the flow of traffic that sped around the castle walls. There was a passageway under the road, but she preferred to take her chances above ground. Waiting for the traffic lights, she found herself beside Jacob Rose. Dinah skipped across in front of him, but as she drew close to the clock tower, she knew that Jacob was gaining on her. She couldn't waste time talking; she had to get on and find Gomer.

"Where are you going, Dinah Jones?" Jacob called.

Dinah hunched into her parka and mumbled, "To meet my mom."

Jacob fell into step beside her. "Why are you limping?"

"I fell over a cat." She realized she'd have to come up with something better before she could escape. "D'you live here or what?" she asked.

"In the castle?" He grinned foolishly, she thought.

"I didn't mean the castle, stupid!"

Jacob Rose compressed his lips, and she felt she shouldn't have called him stupid. It was too late now to make amends, but she'd have to say something if only to take that glum look off his face.

"I saw you in the Castle Arcade, didn't I? I thought you lived down there or something."

"Naw. My auntie's got an apartment on Westgate

Street. I go there when my mom and dad work nights. She's a nurse, and he's in security. He's got a dog an' all."

"Don't you mind half living with someone else?"

"It's great. I've got two families. I'm spoiled rotten!"

This hadn't occurred to her. It was interesting. Before she could ask any more questions, Jacob suddenly ran ahead over the crossing while the light was still green. "Don't get lost," he shouted. "It's getting foggy."

Dinah watched him go, humping a heavy backpack like a coalman, and she found herself wishing that she could have kept him with her just a little longer.

She was right opposite the Angel Hotel now. But suppose Gomer and Rosalie weren't there? She didn't think she could brave the tall glass doors, the thick carpet, and the glossy potted-plant interior to ask for them. Perhaps they were at the theater or the movies. Dinah paced before the clock tower, now and again gazing up at the blue-and-gold clock face and the figures on either side. She saw that one held a shield emblazoned with a scorpion and another was dressed in blue and white and had long golden hair.

She drifted away from the tower, past the lions on either side of the Westgate, and on to the wall where the lioness had her place. Mist swirled along the wall, keeping the animals secret, like creatures hiding in a wilderness. The true lioness would not be there, of course, because she had already found her way into the garden of Griffin's Castle, but perhaps her stony likeness was disguised by the fog. Dinah did not look up. She walked on, toward the bear.

A cold breeze edged around her, and the mist began to lift. The buzz of traffic died away, and Dinah found herself on a deserted street. Every living thing seemed to have vanished; every sound had been silenced. A cloud of leaves flew from the tree behind the wall. They fell about the bear's head in a strange dance. Dinah, who was now close to the bear, felt that his golden eyes were regarding her with great tenderness. Unlike the lioness, who had been content to rest upon the wall, the bear seemed eager to reach Dinah. He was already hunching over the top, his paws sliding down the smooth stone.

"Come on, then," Dinah said.

The bear blinked; his pale weathered nose began to glisten; the dead stone fur took on a rippling golden sheen as he began to heave himself over the wall. Slowly his huge body swung down. Landing on his hind legs, the bear towered above Dinah. The claws that a moment ago had been curled safely beneath his paws now emerged, black and dangerous, from the dense fur.

Dinah stepped back as the bear dropped on all fours. A sound rumbled in his throat, not threatening, but more a questioning sort of grunt, as though he would like to know what Dinah wanted of him.

Dinah smiled delightedly. "Come," she said, turning around with a little dance. And this bright, dancing mood carried her back along the deserted streets.

"What could be better than a bear?" she sang aloud. "A bear to take care of a baby."

He was always there when she looked over her shoulder. His big, surprisingly agile body swung along behind her, and there seemed to be no one about to stare with horror or shout disapproval. They might have been on a snowy road in Alaska, just the two of them, moving through a valley with walls of rock, not houses, on either side and the sky as dark and lonely as the sky above a wilderness.

Only when she was on Anglesey Road did the city begin to wake up. Behind her, far away, the traffic rumbled, and once again the sky was filled with a bleak orange glow.

The bear became more cautious now. He kept close to the wall and moved swiftly between the patches of shadow. Dinah could hear the click of his long claws on the pavement. As they approached Griffin's Castle, she moved near him, taking comfort from his strong, bulky presence.

She could not see the house as she approached. It was entirely hidden behind the evergreens, but as she passed the trees, she was astonished to see lights blazing in the windows. She unlatched the gate and held it wide for the bear to enter. He walked into the garden, his great head rocking, his nose lifted anxiously to catch the drift of unfamiliar scents.

"She's here, too," Dinah murmured.

The lioness appeared at the far end of the garden, but the bear, apart from a wary grunt, did not seem nervous about the other creature. He followed Dinah to the steps, where he sat down heavily and regarded the lioness crouched neatly on the other side.

Two guardians now, Dinah thought happily. She hastened up the steps.

"Hello!" Dinah sprang into the kitchen.

Rosalie screamed, "Where have you been, you little devil?"

"I went to get help," Dinah answered, truly baffled.

"You've been ages!" Rosalie yelled.

"But I thought . . ." In her mind, Dinah swiftly retraced her steps. She had not really been aware of her route home, she realized. She had been so happy in the bear's company, so entranced by the heavy strides and the glow of his thick coat. Perhaps she had danced all the way around the city. This might account for her burning cheeks and the slight ache in her feet.

"Perhaps I got lost," she suggested. "The baby downstairs . . . she . . . didn't die, did she?"

"No, love, she's fine," Rosalie said quietly.

Gomer, sitting beside Rosalie, said, "You should have stayed here. If your mother can't trust you . . ."

"But I had to get help," Dinah burst out. "The baby downstairs was crying. Her mother couldn't warm the milk. She couldn't cook a meal, either, and it was so dark. Luckily, I found a candle. . . . Hey!" She grinned at the lightbulb glowing behind an unfamiliar stained-glass shade. "You fixed it. That's pretty!"

"Yes, I fixed it," Gomer agreed. "The system was overloaded. It blew a fuse, if you can understand what that means. All those heaters in the basement, stupid woman. She might have known."

"How could she?" Dinah clutched Rosalie's shoulder.

"It's an old house, love," her mother explained. "The wiring's not too great."

"You mean it's dangerous." Dinah stared accusingly at Gomer.

"Not if you're careful." He stood up angrily.

"It should be rewired," Dinah persisted. "There's a baby downstairs and a little boy who could easily have an accident. The government's very strict about things like that. The Health and Safety Act —" His expression cut her off.

For a moment Dinah thought he was going to hit her. She was conscious of a terrible violence just below the surface of the tensed knuckles and white fingertips pressed against the table.

Her mother babbled, "Please, Di. You've got to get along with Gomer. It's got to work."

"Shut her up," said Gomer, turning on his heel, "or I will."

It wasn't Rosalie who followed him, but Dinah,

frightened and curious. She wanted to know what the bear and the lioness would do.

They stood beyond the rectangle of light thrown out by the open door. She could just make out the soft sheen of their bodies: the bear to the right of the path, the lioness on the other side, closer to the trees. When Gomer began to descend the steps, the lioness moved restlessly. Dinah stood on the top step, waiting. Gomer walked between the animals without seeing them.

"Get him away from here," Dinah breathed. "Let him know you're wild. Tell him you're with *me!*"

Gomer looked back at her. "What's the matter with you, girl?" he said.

Dinah looked at him with narrowed eyes. The creatures moved toward him, each soundless footstep bringing them closer.

Gomer looked perplexed, uneasy. The two powerful animals were between them now. Gomer caught his breath and wrapped his right arm around himself. At the same moment the bear shoved him sideways and the lioness slashed at his hand. Gomer gasped. He gazed at Dinah, his handsome features all askew.

Rosalie came out and, clinging to Dinah's arm, called, "What is it, Gomer?" She tried to run to him, but Dinah caught her hand and held it tight.

"Don't, Mom. It's dangerous," she whispered.

"Be quiet, Di!" cried Rosalie. "Are you crazy?"

But now Gomer was staggering backward. He turned and ran from the wild beasts that stalked him, flinging himself through the gate and into his car, his eyes averted from the garden.

"Oh, God, what was it?" Rosalie sobbed as Gomer's tires screeched along the curb.

"Breathlessness," said Dinah coldly. "Too many calories and not enough exercise."

"Don't be stupid! Gomer's got a wonderful phy-sique!" Rosalie slumped back into the house.

"Goodnight!" Dinah whispered, looking down on her two champions. "And thank you!"

A MIND AS SHARP AS NEEDLES

Dinah Jones lives on Anglesey Road," Barry announced at breakfast.

"What?" said Mrs. Hughes. "They've all been condemned down there."

"No, they haven't," said Barry. "Not Dinah's house." He spoke quickly, not really believing his own words, remembering the dead facades, the boarded windows, the gardens like untidy pastures, the quiet. "Not all of them," he added.

"It's spooky down there," said Josh through a mouthful of cornflakes. "My friend Harry has seen flickerings in windows and heard bangings in empty houses. Ghosts, he says."

"Squatters!" Kevin corrected. "Anglesey Road is full

of squatters — ask anyone. Isn't it, Dad?" He pulled down his father's newspaper.

His father looked blank, his thoughts still with an article on education. "What?" he said.

"Anglesey Road is full of squatters," Kevin repeated, his new voice changing register like a rusty hinge.

"I wouldn't know."

"What is a condemned house, anyway?" asked Barry, picturing a building behind bars, waiting to die.

"They're not safe, love," said his mother. "Not fit to live in. The shingles are falling off, the boards rotten, that kind of thing."

"They're not all like that," Barry told her. "Dinah's house is sort of . . . beautiful." He remembered the way Dinah had furnished the place, the glowing portraits, the scarlet chaise longue, and the brocade curtains. And the real things, the chandelier and the gilt-framed mirror where the griffin peered down into a pool of shadows. "She calls it a castle!" He ignored

Kevin's snicker and plowed on, aware that his father's newspaper had been neatly folded and that he was now the focus of Mr. Hughes's attention. "She says it was probably called Griffin House once because there was a stone griffin in the grass and another one that's maybe bronze, sitting on a mirror."

"Wait a minute," said Barry's father. "I know who used to live there. Mrs. Iola Gwynne, it's come to me now. There was a bit of a scandal when Mr. Gwynne died. Their son put his mother in a home, said she was funny in the head."

"But if the building was condemned . . ." said Mrs. Hughes.

"Oh, it wasn't then. I'm talking twenty years ago. He rented the place to a couple of families but never did a proper renovation, never maintained it. A disgrace it was. With poor old Mrs. Gwynne fading away in that home down on Roxburgh Street. My mother used to visit her. Lovely woman, she said. Mind as sharp as needles. Just got confused sometimes."

"Well, your mother's been gone ten years," said Mrs. Hughes. "So if Mrs. Gwynne wasn't senile then, she probably is now."

"It's twenty past eight," Mr. Hughes declared, glancing at his watch. "I'm late."

"Forty shopping days to Christmas," Josh reminded his father as he bounded into the hall.

Mr. Hughes groaned and slammed the front door.

Barry raced to school, saving the information about Mrs. Gwynne for Dinah.

He got his opportunity during recess.

"I know something about your house," he told Dinah, proffering his bag of potato chips.

Dinah took one. He could see that she was interested but wasn't going to let him know it. "So what do you know?" she asked casually.

Barry told her about Mrs. Iola Gwynne, the lovely woman with a mind as sharp as needles, fading away in Roxburgh Street. And Dinah immediately saw Mrs. Gwynne as she might have been, in a gown that glittered when she moved and a string of beads that chimed against the gold belt around her hips. Because she would, of course, have been dancing most of the time, with the carpet rolled back, the furniture moved, and the floorboards as smooth as silk under her dancing feet. And sometimes she would have played the harp, sitting in the corner of the long front room. She would have stretched her fingers across the strings, and Griffin's Castle would have been filled with music. . . .

"Dinah!" Barry prodded her. "Are you deaf?"

"What?"

"The bell's rung, and you're not paying attention, are you?"

"Where's Roxburgh Street?" she asked as they walked into school.

"I'm not telling you unless you let me come with you." Actually he didn't know where it was, but he knew what she was going to do.

"You can't," snapped Dinah. "This is between her and me."

Barry didn't speak to Dinah again that day. He was hurt by her harsh words and angry with her ingratitude. He had given her valuable information, and she had just walked away from him.

"Jerk!" he murmured. "Let her stew."

At the end of school, Barry saw Dinah questioning Jacob Rose. Jacob spent his life wandering the different routes between his home and his auntie's apartment close by the castle. He knew nearly every road in the city. Sure enough, Dinah and Jacob walked off together.

"Who cares?" muttered Barry. But he did care. As he walked home, his bag heavy with homework, he resolved to find out just what Dinah intended to do about old Mrs. Gwynne, even if it meant neglecting his homework.

Jacob took Dinah to the end of Roxburgh Street. It was nearly two miles from Elias Road.

"There are hundreds of houses down there," he said. "What number are you looking for?"

"I don't know," Dinah admitted. "It's an old people's home. It'll probably say HOME FOR THE ELDERLY or something like that on the gate, won't it?"

Jacob shrugged. "I'll help," he said.

"I don't need any help."

"I'm going down here, anyway." Jacob began to walk down the street, his shoulders hunched and his strides huge and dogged.

Dinah ran to catch up with him. He couldn't be put off as easily as Barry, she realized. Jacob had been hurt too often to care what she said to him. She had watched him shrug off the teasing. Sometimes he struck out with his feet and fists, but it did him no good. He was always the one to get the blame. He wasn't a gentle giant.

"The lights are up in town," Jacob said. "They're good this year. Loads of stars and trees and stuff.

D'you want to come and see them later? My auntie'll give you your tea."

"Maybe on the weekend," Dinah said.

"Why didn't you ask a friend to come down here with you?"

"I haven't got one," Dinah told him cheerfully.

"Nor me. I don't know why. People laugh at the things I say, but I can't see the joke. And my work's a mess." He paused and glanced at her. "Can you help me with my war project if I wait and come home with you? It'll be dark soon."

"No," Dinah said, adding quickly, "it's Mom, not me. She doesn't like visitors. Ask Barry Hughes. He's clever."

"Not like you." Jacob stopped walking. "I'm not so stupid that I can't tell. You're the cleverest person in the school. There's never been anyone like you. You're astounding, Dinah Jones."

He spoke so fiercely that Dinah was startled. Her

work was not for others to marvel at. She didn't measure it against their achievements. She needed to impress herself and no one else. "I just think it would be better if Barry helped you," she said gently. "You're both kind of alone."

"What about you?" he said.

"It's not the same for me." She hardly knew what she meant by that, for she was alone, except for Rosalie. But she had grown accustomed to this state and was content with it.

They walked on together in silence. It was a busy road, especially at this time, with everyone going home for tea. Jacob scrutinized the numbers on the other side of the street. Dinah took the houses that ran beside her.

"There it is," Jacob said, pointing across the road to an impressive Victorian house. Two brick pillars stood on either side of a wide entrance, and an asphalt drive led up to an oak-paneled front door. There were no flowers beside the drive, no grass, not even a hydrangea bush. But a single tree, bearing deep red berries, leaned over the narrow passage that led around to the back of the house.

"How can you tell that's it?" asked Dinah. If this was the house she wanted, she wasn't sure what to do next.

"Look! Beside the door."

"You've got good eyesight." Dinah could see a bronze plaque nailed to the brick, but she couldn't decipher the words written on it.

"I can't read it from here exactly," Jacob confessed. "But it must be it."

They crossed the road and peered up the drive.

"'St. Garmon's Residential Home,'" Dinah read out.

"Must be it!" Jacob insisted. "D'you want me to come with you?"

"Of course not," Dinah said.

"Hold on a sec!" Jacob leaped down the road. He plucked a handful of pink daisies sprouting from the top of someone else's wall and ran back to Dinah.

"Here," he said, holding them out to her. "For the old person. Old people always like flowers."

"That's stealing," Dinah hissed in a furious whisper. "I don't want anything to do with them."

"Suit yourself!" Jacob turned away. "I'll give them to my auntie."

"Hold on," Dinah called. The flowers had been taken. It was too late to put them back. They might make an old woman happy, and perhaps Dinah's visit would look more official, accompanied by a bouquet.

"I'll take them," she told Jacob as he sauntered back.

He grinned and reached inside his bag. "This'll make them look spiffier," he said, bringing out a scrap of tinfoil. "My sandwiches were in it, but if we make it tidy"— he smoothed the foil against his jacket and wrapped it around the stalks —"she'll like it better."

Dinah took the proffered daisies, now in a neat arrangement. "Thanks," she said.

He hung around the entrance as she walked up the

drive. She could hear him tramping about. "You don't have to wait," she said without looking back.

"Okay."

She glanced around. Jacob Rose had gone, and part of her wished he hadn't.

Dinah pressed a brass doorbell and waited anxiously. She stepped away when the door opened, ready to flee.

A woman in a crisp blue apron smiled down at her. "Hullo!" she said.

Dinah took a deep breath and asked, "Is Mrs. Gwynne here? Mrs. Iola Gwynne? I'm a relative. We've been far away and couldn't come before, but my mother sent these." She held out the flowers.

The woman kept smiling and opened the door wider. Dinah stepped into a well-lit hall. She quickly took in the linoleum floors, the black-framed prints of flowers, a telephone hooked into the wall, and a single upright chair.

"Wait a minute, dear. I'll see if she's ready for visitors." The woman closed the door, took Dinah's flowers, and disappeared down a corridor, reappearing in a few moments with an even brighter smile.

"She might not know you, dear, but it's good for her to have a visitor. Come along." She turned back into the corridor.

Dinah followed. She had not thought it would be like this and felt guilty that she had managed to trespass so easily into someone else's life.

"Here you are!" The woman in blue opened a door into a large room with chairs of different sizes set against the wall. Lights blazed from a high ceiling, the floor was carpeted in dark brown, and a gas fire glowed beneath an ornate wooden mantelpiece. The heat was stifling.

"She's over by the window!" said the woman, but somehow Dinah already knew Mrs. Iola Gwynne. There were about a dozen people in the room. Some gazed silently into nowhere, and others murmured softly to themselves or to one another. Mrs. Gwynne sat with her back to the window, not bent or leaning like some of the old people. She had small, stern features and loosely curled white hair. Her clothes were lavender colored, and she wore a single strand of pearls around her neck. There was a small table beside her and an empty chair on the other side. Someone had put the daisies in a vase, and Dinah observed that they matched, exactly, the scarf draped across Mrs. Gwynne's shoulders.

Dinah couldn't bring herself to kiss the powdered cheek, and shaking hands seemed far too formal, so she took the empty chair and rested her elbow on the table.

They sat regarding each other across the flowers until Mrs. Gwynne spoke. She had a surprisingly clear voice, as light and tuneful as a young woman's. "I don't know you," she said.

"No," Dinah confessed. "But I live in your house, so I thought I'd come and visit you." She gave a bright smile.

Mrs. Gwynne didn't return it. Dinah had the uncanny feeling that the old woman could see beyond the smile and was looking through Dinah into the house that had once been hers. Dinah longed to know if she had guessed right about the brocade curtains, the bright carpets and furniture, and especially the harp.

"I don't have a house," said Mrs. Gwynne.

"Yes, you do," said Dinah. "I call it Griffin's Castle because of the griffins. They are griffins, aren't they? There was one in the garden and another one perched on a great mirror. It's all patchy now, the mirror, but the griffin is looking into it like this," and Dinah leaned forward, tucking in her chin to study the buttons on her parka. "Why are they there, the griffins? Who chose them?"

Mrs. Gwynne stared at Dinah in astonishment. Then, quite without warning, she opened her mouth and laughed, so high and so loud, it shook the room and all of its occupants into life. "It was a mistake," she cried. "What a joke!"

"A mistake," Dinah murmured in dismay. She tried not to look at the faces turned in her direction.

"Yes." Mrs. Gwynne leaned across the table. "They should have been dragons. My grandfather ordered them from a Mr. Nicholls in 1890, when he was carving those creatures for the castle wall. My grandfather was a very proud man. 'The marquess can have lions on *his* gate,' he said. 'But *I* shall have dragons.'"

"I see," said Dinah. "So why are there griffins?"

"It was a mistake." Mrs. Gwynne politely covered her giggles with a white hand. "The griffins arrived, you see, all beautifully carved and ready, and there was to be a grand dinner at the house, and no dragons could be found in time. So my grandfather kept the griffins. I wasn't there, you understand, but my father was. He told me all about it when I was, oh, very small." Mrs. Gwynne tilted her head and gazed into the distance with a smile.

Dinah clasped her hands in her lap. She was disappointed that the griffins were a mistake. Perhaps she had pictured everything wrong, and there had been no Persian carpets, no portraits, and no harp. She had to know. "Did you play the harp, Mrs. Gwynne?" she asked.

The old woman gazed at her pale, rather elegant hands in a puzzled way, and then she turned to Dinah and said, "My father died in the Great War, 1918, at the very end. My mother told me that he had a charmed life and would live forever." Her pale blue eyes grew cold and flinty. She looked so angry. It might have been yesterday when they told her that her father would never come home. "I have his letters," she continued in a confidential tone. "My mother gave them to me. He knew a poet called Wilfred Owen. He died, too. They were all so young. It was the wire. Whenever I think of wire, I think of death."

"Wire?" said Dinah, puzzled.

"Barbed wire," said Mrs. Gwynne through clenched teeth. "They fell on the wire, you see, and couldn't move. The guns ripped them to pieces while they hung there."

Dinah shuddered. She searched for an appropriate response and found herself saying, "Rudyard Kipling's son died in that war. I love his books. He had a Rolls-Royce and drove like a fiend." She glanced at Mrs. Gwynne, who was looking puzzled, but as Dinah talked on, the old woman's expression changed to interest and then wonderment.

"I love it," Mrs. Gwynne suddenly declared. "*The Jungle Book*! I can see it all. Father wolf caught in mid-air as he is about to pounce on little Mowgli. But the mother is my favorite. She's the one they're all afraid of." And all at once Mrs. Gwynne left her chair and paced about the room, quoting effortlessly from her favorite book.

Dinah was astonished at the old woman's memory. She felt as though she had accidentally pressed the switch that jerked Mrs. Gwynne to life. Everyone in the room was staring at her now. An elderly man in slippers and an outdoor coat began to clap. "Well done!" he called out. His companion muttered, "Shut up!" and someone else began to moan.

Dinah shrank into her chair, trying to make herself as small as possible. She was rather embarrassed by Mrs. Gwynne's unself-conscious and spirited performance.

But Mrs. Gwynne carried on, her head held high, every moment becoming louder and more confident. Now she began to add gestures. "Akela, the great gray lone wolf, who protects the boy and loves him. He misses his kill and knows he must leave the pack and walk alone forever."

The door opened, and the woman in blue walked over to Mrs. Gwynne. "Sit down, dear," she said.

"No, Betty, let me finish," cried Mrs. Gwynne.

A man came in, wearing a jacket in the same shade of blue as Betty's smock. He took Mrs. Gwynne's arm and began to lead her to the door.

"Leave her alone," said the old man who had applauded.

"You're upsetting people, Mrs. Gwynne," Betty said quietly.

"Nonsense," objected Mrs. Gwynne as the man maneuvered her through the door.

"You'd better go, dear," Betty told Dinah. She left Mrs. Gwynne to the man in the blue jacket and led Dinah to the front door. "Don't worry, love. She's just excited. You've probably done her a bit of good."

"Of course I played the harp," Mrs. Gwynne's voice sang out in the distance.

Betty smiled. "Come again," she said.

Dinah walked down the asphalt drive. Roxburgh Street was quieter now. Everyone had gone home. Behind the curtained windows, Dinah imagined bright, cozy kitchens, toast and jam, and cakes fresh from the oven.

Griffin's Castle would be cold. Her mother might already have left the house, but the rooms would not be empty. There *had* been a harp. She would stand in the long room and see it as it was, with a blazing chandelier and gleaming furniture.

Perhaps they would spend Christmas Day in the Harp Room. They would have a log fire and a tree where the harp had stood. Christmas as it should be. Not as it had been at Gran's, all cold looks and arguments. Not in a drafty hostel or crammed into a tiny studio. Not in the park, eating french fries from a bag, like last year.

Mrs. Gwynne would come back to Griffin's Castle, and in the evening, they would read aloud from *The Jungle Book.*

Dinah sped home, humming a carol.

The cat was waiting for her beside the gate.

"What is it with you?" said Dinah. "Don't you belong anywhere?"

How could she have known that they belonged together?

JACOB AND THE WALL

"Did you see her then?" Barry croaked over Dinah's shoulder.

They were shuffling into assembly.

"Yes," Dinah said.

"And was her mind as sharp as needles?"

"Sharper. She knows all about the Great War, that's the first one. She's got her father's letters. She can tell me a lot, about the wire and the trenches. I think I'll go back and talk to her."

"But that isn't the war —"

"Quiet at the back!" called Mr. Williams.

Barry fell silent. Their project should have been on WW II, not WW I. Had Dinah forgotten? It wasn't like her. Didn't she care? Barry was tempted not to tell

Dinah. His mark would be higher if she wrote about the wrong war.

At break he was approached by Jacob Rose. He tried to escape into a crowd of boys, but Jacob bore down on him with a determined frown. He offered Barry a chunk of cake wrapped in cellophane.

"What's that for?" Barry drew away as though the offering was poisoned.

"I don't need it," Jacob said.

"Nor do I," Barry declared.

"Can I ask you something?"

Barry felt nervous standing in the tall boy's shadow. Jacob had wide fists that had damaged even the most robust boys. "What?" he asked.

"I can't do my history project."

"So?"

"I thought you could help me, like."

Barry swung a foot, feeling trapped. He was afraid of what the fists would do if he refused, but to be considered Jacob's friend was even worse. Smelly Rose, they sometimes called him, though today that didn't seem to apply.

"Ask Dinah," Barry said, looking toward the classroom window where Dinah sat working. She'd been given the task of writing a letter to the local paper.

Jacob gazed at Dinah's absorbed figure for a moment, then thrust his hands in his pockets and walked away.

Barry didn't know what to think. He was relieved to have escaped Jacob's attentions, but the gangly boy's submissiveness made him feel uncomfortable.

He didn't have another chance to ask Dinah about Mrs. Gwynne. After school she slipped away so quickly, he never saw her. He considered walking down to Anglesey Road, but then thought better of it.

When tea was over, Josh and Kevin kicked a soccer ball around the back garden. Barry watched them through the window, his pallid reflection superimposed on Kevin's broad frame.

"Why don't you join them, love?" his mother asked.

"It's dark out there, and I've got homework," Barry said. "Can I go to the shop for some more paper?"

"No farther, then. And straight back."

"It'll take me half an hour. I've got to choose the right stuff, and there might be a line." He would have to run, he realized, if he were to get to Dinah's house and be back in half an hour.

He raced up to his room, tucked a notebook into his parka, and slipped out of the house.

It was dark when he reached Anglesey Road. In just a week, night skies had taken over in the afternoons. Now only a few leaves clung to the sycamores along the road. But the wind was soft and surprisingly warm. The frozen mist in Dinah's garden came as a shock.

Barry couldn't see the ground beneath the rows of lofty evergreens, but something moved there, something silent and heavy. The light in the top window of the house seemed to float in a kind of never-never land. Barry fixed his eyes on it, too afraid to bring his gaze back to where the phantoms roamed. Dinah's voice, close to his ear, nearly knocked him off his feet.

"What are you doing here?" She was on the other side of the wall, but he hadn't seen the door open or heard her approach.

Barry swallowed and nodded at the window. "I thought you were up there! I didn't see you in the garden."

"There's no one in. No one at all. My friend Tahira is supposed to be baby-sitting me, but she's out. Probably gone to get something for the baby. I left the light on so the house wouldn't look empty."

"I'll come in if you're scared," Barry offered.

"Of course I'm not scared. I've got . . ." She stopped.

"A guard dog?" he asked hopefully.

"Sort of."

"What, then?" He could have sworn a bulky shape moved behind Dinah. But what was it? Something told him that it was not human.

"There are two of them," Dinah said. "A bear and a lioness."

"What?" Barry's mouth fell open. "Are they . . . from a circus or something?"

"They're from the wall!" It seemed to be a challenge.

"What wall?" he asked, mystified.

"Around the castle. You must know. The animal wall."

Barry wavered between horror and incredulity. "But they're made of stone," he said huskily.

"Made? Yes . . . and they are stone, of course," she said warily. "But after dark they come here. They're going to stop him."

"Who?"

"Gomer Gwynne. He's doing his best to separate Mom and me, and he's letting Griffin's Castle fade away. But the animals will frighten him off."

She spoke so simply that Barry almost found

himself believing her. But how could he? "Is this a joke?" he said.

"No! I don't expect you to believe me, but I'd like you to. I haven't told anyone else. I thought you might be able to accept this kind of thing, Barry."

Again that brisk, truthful delivery. He felt flattered but extremely worried. "I'd better go," he said.

She didn't seem to be offended. "Why are you here, anyway?" she asked.

For a moment, Barry couldn't remember. He covered his confusion with a few chesty coughs. At last it came to him. "Mrs. Gwynne," he said. "You never told me what happened, not properly, anyway. And I did tell you where she was."

"No, you didn't. You tried to blackmail me," she said.

A car was coming down the road. It rolled toward them, sleek and black, slowing as it approached. Dinah watched it anxiously. The car stopped behind Barry, and someone got out. It was the man who had swept into Griffin's Castle on Barry's first visit — Gomer Gwynne.

Gomer hardly noticed the boy this time, but bore down on Dinah with a grim expression. Dinah backed away.

A very pretty woman got out of the car and called, "Di!" as Dinah ran toward the house.

Barry watched Dinah's flight through the misty garden, the tall man pursuing her, and the woman running behind him in delicate red shoes. Surely she was too young to be Dinah's mother. She didn't even look like her. Barry felt as though he were watching a scene from a movie with the sound turned down, for everything was muffled except the tapping of the woman's shoes. It was so dark in there.

And then Dinah opened the front door, flooding the scene with light. Barry, turning away, was suddenly arrested by Dinah's voice. She was standing at the top of the steps, as rigid as a soldier. "Where are you?"

she called, and her voice, clear and startling, halted the man.

Something extraordinary happened to Gomer then. He recoiled, flung up his hand, and crashed to the ground.

Dinah vanished as the woman ran forward crying, "Gomer!"

Barry ran. He had seen enough. There *was* a creature in Dinah's garden, perhaps two. He had to believe her now. *But how had it happened? How had she brought two stone creatures to life?* Barry's fists were clenched against his aching chest. "I didn't see them," he wheezed. "She told me, and I believed. That's not the same thing at all."

He was still arguing with himself when he stumbled through his own front door. He stood in the hall, trying to get his breath back, comforted by the familiar clamor of his home: the TV blaring, Josh yelling at someone, the dishwasher humming in the kitchen — friendly, reassuring noise.

He called out, "I'm back, Mom," as he mounted the stairs.

His mother was arguing with Josh. "I can't be in two places at once," she complained.

It struck a chord in Barry's head. *Can't be in two places at once!* Of course not. It's against the law of nature. If the animals were in Dinah's garden, then they couldn't be on the castle wall. Someone would notice. There'd be an outcry, a mention in the paper or on the television news. He rushed downstairs again.

"Did you see the news, Mom?" he asked breathlessly.

Josh was sitting at the kitchen table, looking glum. Mrs. Hughes bent over him and spelled out *physician* very slowly.

"Thanks," Josh mumbled.

"So did you?" Barry asked again.

Mrs. Hughes brushed back a lock of hair. "Did I what?"

"Watch the news, Mom?"

"I haven't had time," she said.

"Well, it might have been yesterday or last week. Have you heard anything about the animals on the castle wall? That they've been stolen or vanished or, or . . . anything?"

His mother and brother stared at him, wearing identical frowns.

"What's the panic, love?" Mrs. Hughes said gently. "Have you seen them prowling the streets?"

Josh giggled, and his mother joined in with an apologetic sort of titter. Barry sloped off, feeling ridiculous.

It was too late to visit the wall. How could he find out? He knew no one who lived down in the city center. And then he remembered Jacob Rose.

The phone book. Barry pulled the heavy book from a pile of magazines on the hall table. "Darn!" he grunted. Jacob's aunt would have a different name. It wouldn't be Rose because she was married to a foreigner. Barry remembered because Jacob had brought a photograph of his uncle's home to school. It was a rather grand building, and everyone had laughed. "Poland!" Barry exclaimed aloud. "That's where it was." He wished he had paid more attention at the time. Barry went back into the kitchen. Josh's work didn't seem to have progressed.

"P . . . H . . ." Mrs. Hughes repeated wearily.

"You know Jacob Rose?" Barry interrupted. "Well, you know he sometimes stays with his aunt. . . ."

"Mrs. Stokowski?" His mother's eyes didn't leave Josh's book for an instant.

"Mom, you're a genius," cried Barry. "How did you know?"

"Everyone knows Mrs. Stokowski, love. She plays the piano for the old folks at the institute."

"Thanks, Mom!" Barry would have hugged her if it had been possible to reach past Josh and his mess on the table. "You're the greatest!"

"I don't know what I've done," she said as he sped off again.

There were only two Stokowskis in the book. One

was a delicatessen. So it had to be Mr. T. Stokowski. Barry dialed the number. He was surprised when Jacob answered the phone, but keeping cool, he asked, "Mrs. Stokowski?"

"I'll get her," Jacob muttered. At the end of the line, the receiver clonked onto something hard.

"No!" Barry shouted. "Jacob! Jacob! Jacob?"

The receiver was lifted again, and a bemused voice said, "Yes?"

"It's me, Barry," said Barry, feeling foolish. "Barry Hughes."

"Barry?" Jacob's telephone voice was deep and rather flat.

"Yes. I'm calling about the history project. I'll help you if you do something for me."

"What?"

Barry could not discern a hint of pleasure in Jacob's tone.

"Can you go and look at the wall for me? The animal wall by the castle?"

"What for?" Jacob didn't even sound surprised.

Barry began to regret his call. His request sounded ridiculous, and he couldn't bring himself to tell Jacob the truth. "I just wanted to know how many animals there were. It's for an essay I'm writing."

"Okay. D'you want me to go now? Shall I call you back?"

"No, not now, if you're having tea. But soon, before morning, anyway. While it's still dark. You can tell me tomorrow, and I'll help you with your project at lunchtime."

"Thanks!" Jacob jammed the receiver back on its cradle, amazed by his good fortune. Looking at the castle wall seemed such a simple task.

"For you, was it, love?" His aunt seemed pleased for him. He had never had a phone call before. He knew she worried about him. Schoolwork wasn't easy for him, nor was making friends.

"It was my friend Barry," he told her. "He said he'd help me with my history."

"He's a good friend then, Jacob." Uncle Tadeusz winked across the table. "Going to watch the boxing with me tonight?"

Auntie Mair clicked her tongue, and Jacob said, "'Course!" The wall could wait for half an hour.

But the boxing lasted for an hour, and then there was the news, and then a film about the American Civil War. Uncle Tadeusz loved television. Auntie Mair popped her head around the door twice and suggested that Jacob should go to bed, but his uncle said, "Go on with you, woman. This is history. Jacob's learning something." Which wasn't exactly true because no dates or places were mentioned. As far as Jacob could tell, it was all revenge and romance. But his uncle wanted to share the excitement with someone, and it wasn't Auntie Mair's cup of tea at all.

Jacob fell asleep before the film drew to its gory and predictable conclusion. Uncle Tadeusz woke him with a gentle shake. "Jacob, I'm sorry, boy. You'd better get to bed before your auntie finds you here."

His uncle turned out the lights and crept away with a guilty smile and a warning finger to his lips.

When Jacob got into bed, he was still half asleep and forgot to draw his curtains. An hour later moonlight spilled onto his face, and suddenly he was wide awake. He remembered Barry. He stared at the moon, wondering what to do. Every minute that passed was taking Barry's promised help further away. Jacob could lie awake all night, but if he didn't do something, if he didn't go and count the animals, it would be too late.

"Before morning," Barry had said. "While it's still dark!" *Why?* Jacob wondered. *What was the difference? What happened to the stone creatures at night?* Now burning with curiosity, Jacob dressed hurriedly.

He checked the two keys in his pocket and tiptoed downstairs. The building was silent, and when he pulled the front door shut behind him, the click of the big lock sounded like a shot.

It was cold outside. The pavement glittered, and Jacob's breath condensed in soft clouds. He hunched himself deep into his parka as he approached Castle Street and the animal wall. He was not afraid of being out alone so late, but his scalp tingled expectantly. He had never known such quiet.

He reached the end of Westgate Street, turned a corner, and found himself facing the wall on the other side of Castle Street. Before him sat the pelican; next came the anteater. They looked as they always had, friendly and unremarkable. Farther along the wall sat two raccoons, a leopard, a beaver, and a vulture. Nothing special about them, though he had always found the leopard rather menacing. The vulture was not an unattractive bird. It was rather grand, in fact. Beyond the vulture, Jacob could make out two apes and a hyena, and as he moved along parallel with the wall, he saw a seal, riding the crest of stone as though it were a wave.

Jacob had counted eleven animals, but he knew there were more. Nearer to the clock tower, the trees formed a shadowy thicket, and it was hard to make out what lay beneath. Jacob realized he would have to walk closer, but he was reluctant to do so. He was shivering violently, and although he told himself that this was due to the cold air, he knew that it was not entirely true. A frozen mist clung to the end of the wall, and he was afraid to look into it.

"I must," he said aloud and took several determined paces forward. If only he could remember the animals that were hidden by the mist, he could pretend that he had counted them. *There's a bear somewhere*, he thought. *And a lioness and a lynx around the corner.*

He began to count again, tapping freezing fingers against his palms as he stepped closer to the dense white mist. His teeth rattled against one another, and he couldn't keep his lips closed. The cold air bit into his skull and made him dizzy. Trees, tower, and sky began to spin. Jacob tried to focus on the mist, but his desperate gaze couldn't penetrate the thick snowy blanket.

And now he found that he couldn't move at all. He seemed to be held prisoner in an endless winter night.

His imagination ran riot. He began to detect a movement in the mist. Something dropped from the wall and ran away, fast. It was gray and sleek.

As Jacob watched, rigid with disbelief, a hand touched his shoulder, and he screamed. The man behind him gave a grunt of shock and said, "What are you doing here, boy?"

Jacob was so relieved to see a real person, he smiled foolishly and said, "I'm watching for something," adding, for good measure, "an owl, as a matter of fact."

"D'you know what time it is?" the policeman asked.

Jacob squinted up at the clock tower. "Can't see," he said. The gold hands pointed quite clearly to two o'clock, but Jacob didn't want to believe them.

The policeman swore and asked, "Where d'you live, then?"

Jacob nodded toward Westgate Street. "Down there," he said.

"Isn't anyone at home?"

"Yes," Jacob said. "They're asleep."

"You'd better get back there fast, boy. And don't let me catch you out at this time again."

"No, sir," Jacob said, and ran.

Before he walked up the steps to the flat, Jacob glanced back. The policeman stood, unmoving, at the end of the road. His features could not be seen beneath the peak of his hat, but Jacob knew that he was watching him and that the policeman would still be patrolling the area long after Jacob had fallen asleep.

No one heard him let himself in. Behind a door Uncle Tadeusz grunted and whistled like a train. How could Auntie Mair sleep with that racket going on? Perhaps she was used to it.

Jacob's room lay at the end of a corridor. When he closed his door, his uncle's relentless snore could not be heard. It was not a noise that kept Jacob awake until dawn; it was the picture in his head of a cold cloud that hugged a castle wall and the sleek flight of a creature made of stone.

THE WOLF

Dinah did not attempt to sleep. Still fully dressed, she paced her brightly papered room, trying to keep at bay the little clouds of anger that kept muddling her thoughts.

She must keep a cool head. She had to find a way to slice through Gomer's plan. It must be cut into tiny pieces. Banished. He was going to take Rosalie away; it was as plain as the long bony nose on his face.

Dinah's creatures had hurt him. There was no doubt about it. They had jostled and pushed and frightened him, but they had not driven him away. He had slumped in the kitchen with her mother's arms around his neck and hot tea steaming by his hand, and he had stared at Dinah as though she were a ghost. But he couldn't say a word, for it was something quite outside the understanding of a man like Gomer Gwynne, a man who dealt in commodities and balance sheets, in property and wages and customer satisfaction.

He had touched the rough hair of wild animals. He had smelled them, felt their awful energy. But he could never tell a soul. How could he say, "A bear nearly throttled me. A lioness knocked me to the ground and would have eaten me"? It was impossible.

And it had not worked.

Rosalie was consumed with love and sympathy, and this had given Gomer a smug sort of power. It hadn't taken long for him to recover from the animals' attack.

"Don't you dare go to that home again, d'you hear!" he snarled at Dinah.

She knew very well what he meant. "Why not?" she said. "Mrs. Gwynne was very pleased to see me."

"So I've heard."

"It did her good, they said."

"They said, did they? Well, I know better."

"But why —"

Gomer brought his hand down, hard and flat on the table. The teacup jumped, and liquid spilled in a stream onto the floor. "Because I say so. Isn't that enough? Rosalie, for God's sake, tell her."

"Dinah, love . . ."

But Dinah would not be told. "She's a lonely old lady. I didn't do any harm. I just talked to her for a bit. You should visit her more often."

When Gomer swore, he did so with relish, his lips curled back like an angry dog. "Girl, she doesn't even know who I am!"

This threw Dinah momentarily, but she could not be deflected. "So what? She can still be happy even if she doesn't know exactly what's going on. She can talk about *The Jungle Book* and her harp and the dragons that should have been outside your door."

"Enough!" he blazed. "You won't see her again. That's final."

"I will! I will!" cried Dinah, looking at her mother's blanched face, trying to catch her eye.

"You do so at your peril, girl!" He stood up, shaking Rosalie off his arm.

Dinah jumped back. She knew Gomer would have hit her if her mother hadn't been there. "You're an awful man," she growled through clenched teeth. "A horror!" And she stormed out, making an unnecessary clatter on the stairs. But when she reached the first landing, she slipped off her shoes and crept down, barefoot, to hear what Gomer said.

The kitchen door was open just a crack, enough to let a thread of sound into the hall. Dinah wondered if Gomer would dare to tell Rosalie that invisible animals roamed the garden. But all he said was, "Rosalie, oh, Rosalie, come away with me!" His voice was like silk.

"Gomer, you know I want to, but"— Dinah could feel her mother's hesitation —"but there's Dinah. I know she shouldn't have gone to the home without asking. But was it wrong, really? I mean, she didn't do any harm, did she?"

"I don't want my mother talking about the house."

Gomer's voice lost some of its silkiness. "I don't want her remembering. I put her in that place for her own good. She was a danger to herself — left fires on, let the bath overflow, locked herself out." Irritation crept into his voice. "The house was too big for her to manage. . . ."

"Couldn't you find anyone to look after her?" Rosalie asked gently.

"I chose not to." He began to sound impatient. "The house is falling down, anyway, so it was for the best. Mind you, she drove us all mad at first, talking and complaining, making me out to be a monster. Then gradually she forgot about the house and me. Forgot everything. She's calmer now, easier to handle. I don't visit her because she doesn't know me. It's best for everyone. So tell Dinah to lay off, and we'll all be happy."

All? Dinah wanted to shout. She remembered the sudden liveliness in the pale blue eyes and the way Mrs. Gwynne had gazed at her own hand as though she had just discovered it.

"So will you come, Rosie?" Gomer wheedled. "Come to Scotland for Christmas. Think of it: log fires, snowy nights, dancing in the dark."

"Oh, Gomer . . ."

"I want the best for you, Rosalie!"

Dinah was waiting for Rosalie's answer.

"What about Dinah?" Rosalie said.

"Surely there must be *somewhere*," Gomer groaned, "somewhere she can go. Her gran, her aunt, someone will take her."

Dinah walked softly away.

She sat on her bed and tried to read, but the sense of the story slid away from her. She kept remembering how she had tried, that Christmas three years ago, to be a part of Gran's family. There was an edgy atmosphere in the house even before Dinah had caused it to deteriorate completely. Auntie June and Uncle John had come from Hereford with Dinah's cousins, Angela and Julie. Granddad, with his watery eyes, could only talk about his garden, and Uncle John, who didn't like gardens, kept winking at his precious girls and making them giggle. They had been sitting around a table covered with good things, party poppers and scarlet napkins, holly tied with ribbons, and the turkey, of course. And Dinah had tried to explain how the muscle fibers in a turkey change shape irreversibly when heated above 104°F and why overcooking led to tough meat. She then went on to tell them how some turkey suppliers tried to tenderize their birds by injecting them with fat. She had thought this would be interesting to the family, but everyone had fallen silent, and then her cousin Angela, who was the same age as Dinah, whimpered, "Shut her up, Mom! Shut her up!" Then she and her sister, Julie, had started to cry.

For some reason everyone considered that Dinah had purposely caused Angela's distress, and Auntie June screamed at Rosalie, "Get that kid out of here. She's not going to make my girls cry at Christmastime."

So Dinah had spent the day in a cold room upstairs, listening to the distant crackle of wrapping paper and the exclamations of delight and surprise.

When Rosalie came to fetch her down, Dinah wouldn't go. And she wouldn't touch the cold turkey and clammy mince pies that were sent up later. "I haven't done anything wrong," she said. "They just don't like me, Mom."

It was then that her mother had tried to explain Gran's attitude. How Rosalie had always been the favorite until she had a baby and her young husband had run away. "Gran begged me to give you up, have you adopted. She wanted me to start again, take my exams, have a good life. But I couldn't, Di. I loved you more than Gran, and she could never forgive me for that."

"Nor me for being born," said Dinah.

And Rosalie had hugged her tight, saying, "Oh, Dinah, I wish you weren't clever."

Dinah didn't mean to be. She just knew things.

They were there in her head: facts and figures, continents and constellations. The world was filled with interesting things, but no one, it seemed, wanted to understand them.

Dinah turned on Rosalie's radio and tried to drown herself in music, but she could not escape the voices in her head. *What about Dinah? WHAT ABOUT DINAH?*

At length she switched off the radio and shouted, "Gomer Gwynne is my mortal enemy!" It cleared her head a little.

Outside a car roared to life and sped away. There was no mistaking Gomer's Audi. Two floors down, Rosalie prepared to go to bed. The water pipes gurgled, and a door closed. She didn't come up to say good night.

What about Dinah? WHAT ABOUT DINAH?

"Time for Dinah to take care of herself," Dinah murmured.

She had come to realize, just lately, that she and Rosalie were somehow changing places. Soon she would be taller than her mother and stronger. Already she knew more about the world than Rosalie would ever know. And yet Dinah did not feel quite ready to be alone.

"Why couldn't you wait, Mom?" she whispered bitterly. "Why did Gomer have to come along?"

Dinah put on her coat and left the room. She carried her shoes, but the stairs still creaked. She had tried to learn their pattern and avoid the bad treads, but there was always a new squeak. The rot was spreading. To Dinah the groaning boards sounded thunderous. But Rosalie slept on.

So they're going to knock you down, are they? Dinah thought. *We'll see about that!*

She let herself out the front door, closed it softly behind her, and put on her shoes.

On either side of Dinah, the evergreens surged toward the sky. They looked denser somehow and seemed to be bristling with secrets.

"Where are you?" Dinah called.

The bear appeared first. He shook his great head and gave a strange little grunt as he approached Dinah. The frozen grass made a soft crunching noise under his big feet.

Dinah had never touched him before. She was almost afraid that her hand might not find him, that she might reach into empty air and discover that he was only an illusion. Now she put out her hand and felt the thick soft fur between his ears.

The trees behind her rustled, and when she looked around, the lioness emerged, her eyes glowing with an eerie brilliance. She came and sat close to Dinah, and, confident of touching her, the girl extended her free hand and laid it on the golden head. A sound rippled beneath her fingers. The lioness was purring.

"I must go now," Dinah said. "Will you come?"

The animals gazed at her, suddenly solemn.

"I don't know where I'm going," Dinah said, frowning with concentration. "I've just got to think. I've got to find a way to stop Gomer Gwynne. Maybe the solution's out there." She was speaking to herself now as she looked beyond the evergreens to the hazy light in the street.

The animals followed her down the path. The gate was swollen with frost and wouldn't open. It was not only the frost that held it fast. Dinah sensed another strength battling against her. She didn't want to believe it, but something told her that the animals were trying to keep her in the garden. And for the first time Dinah felt alarmed by their mysterious power. She had thought they would support her in everything, but it was not so. There was something outside the gate they did not want her to reach.

"But I must," said Dinah, even though she didn't know why it was suddenly so imperative for her to get through the gate.

She braced herself on the path and tugged at the wood with all her strength. The gate gave with a crack, but opened no wider than a foot. Dinah slipped through.

Before she walked away, she felt compelled to look back. The bear and the lioness were watching her from the wall, and Dinah felt a little shiver of apprehension. There was something menacing in their attitude and the force of their bright gaze.

She began to run. Anglesey Road stretched interminably before her, and she never seemed to gain any ground. It was almost as though the creatures in the garden were holding her back. She might run forever and never get anywhere.

The pavement was laced with the twisting shadows of naked trees, and the overgrown hedges crackled with cold. And gradually Dinah gave in to a terrible foreboding of the unseen dangers that might lie ahead. Her footsteps slowed until she stood motionless in the hostile night. She was about to turn back when she saw movement in a pool of light and a cat appeared, walking toward her. Dinah knew, even from a distance, that it was the same shabby animal that waited by her gate. Its glinting eyes and the motion of its soft white feet gave her an uncanny surge of hope. When it met Dinah's gaze, the cat stopped for a moment, then arched its back and bounded away. And Dinah followed, determined not to let it out of her sight.

The cat vanished around a corner, and she pursued it tenaciously. Every time she thought she had lost it, the cat would reappear and wait for her to get closer before running off again. This happened so frequently that Dinah became quite certain the cat was deliberately leading her somewhere.

"You're not mine," she called breathlessly, "so where are you taking me?"

The cat seemed to hear this, for it halted abruptly and looked back at her. This time it waited until she was beside it, and then it slipped through the palings of an iron gate. Dinah made to follow but hesitated when she saw what lay beyond.

Tombstones like stunted trees stood in rows, their shadows black as pits: moon-bleached slabs of marble, lichen-covered crosses, urns, and monuments to lost soldiers, all overlooked by broad unbending yews.

Dinah shivered and hugged herself for comfort. She could not go in there at night.

The cat looked back at her as it crept deeper into the world of silent bones.

"Oh, no, I won't go in there," said Dinah and turned away. But such an insistent wail drifted from the graveyard, she couldn't ignore it.

She lifted the heavy latch, and the gate swung back. It closed behind her with a dreadful clang that seemed to hang in the still cold air for minutes. As she walked up the gravel path, she could hear her heart drumming furiously in her head.

The cat left the path and began to weave through the maze of graves. Dinah watched its swift, confident movements. It was no longer a scarred and scruffy creature. Moonlight gave the cat a grace and dignity that was not usually apparent. Dinah began to follow it.

When the cat moved into the shadow of a wide yew tree, Dinah lost it. She felt suddenly alone and frightened, surrounded by the dark and silent tombs, and longed to rush back to the gate, but something held her where she was. She looked down slowly and found the cat only a few feet away. It was crouched in a neat hollow beside a gravestone, almost buried in dead grass and weeds. Dinah could see that the great slab of granite under the tree afforded some protection against the weather. The cat *lived* there. She leaned closer but did not want to touch the animal. It seemed mysterious and unnatural huddled there so close to the dead. But she could not leave it.

Now she noticed that the headstone was different from the others. It was thicker and roughly hewn, like a rock that had thrust its way through the earth, and it was veined with quartz as though fingers of lightning had been trapped there forever. It was the most beautiful thing that Dinah had ever seen. As she ran her hand over its cool surface, she could almost believe the stone held a strong and compassionate spirit that was trying to soothe her. And she had a fleeting image of the rock where it truly belonged, high on a white mountain with only the wind for company.

The front of the headstone had been polished smooth, and when Dinah knelt to look for a name, she found the carved inscription: OLWEN, BELOVED WIFE OF TOMOS GWALCHMAI. BORN 12TH FEBRUARY 1912. DIED 1ST DECEMBER 1937.

"Cat," exclaimed Dinah, "you have found my great-grandmother!"

Beneath the date were the Welsh words

Y COLLI YN DRISTWCH

Y COFIO'N DDIDDANWCH

"'Loss is sad, memory a consolation,'" Dinah murmured in a somewhat imperfect translation.

She leaned forward to touch the cat's soft head in a gesture of gratitude, but before she could do so, a distant sound froze her hand. It was the sort of howl that could only have been made by something wild and dangerous.

The cat immediately leaped from its bed, its ears flattened and its teeth bared in a guttural snarl. It glared into the dark, angry and fearful. Dinah was more afraid of the cat than of the distant howl. She ran from the grave and the gruesome animal.

The dry hedge rattled as the gate clanged behind her.

Dinah, bounding over the paving stones, soon realized that she was going in the wrong direction. Nothing was familiar. But if she was getting closer to the city, where was it?

The ground became soft and her footfalls muffled. Houses vanished and branches closed above her head like the arched timbers of a great cathedral. There was no horizon, nothing but the moon, as cold and pale as a pool of ice.

And, as she ran, she became aware of other footsteps, almost silent but still there, just out of reach, matching her own. An animal moved into the path of moonlight and came running toward her. Its pointed ears and loping stride could have been those of a dog. But it was not a dog. With a shudder of recognition, Dinah whispered, "Wolf!"

DINAH'S GARDEN

The wind was bitter, and a cloud the color of a dark bruise rolled above the flat school roof. Jacob stood with the wind in his face, as close to the door as possible. He could hardly keep his eyes open. He wanted Barry to make the first move.

His fingers worked away in his pockets, ticking off the animals one by one. "Six, seven, eight, nine, ten," he murmured. There were two raccoons, but they sat close enough to be treated as a single creature.

"Counting sheep, Jacob Rose?" asked Mrs. Price. "You look as though you're still asleep."

Jacob shook his head, lost count, and started again. "Ten," he repeated to himself as Mrs. Price walked away. She picked up a potato chip bag and tapped someone on the shoulder.

Barry approached. "Did you do it, then?" he asked. He was acting casual, but Jacob could tell he was burning with curiosity.

Jacob nodded. "Ten," he said. "Twelve if you count the two lions with shields at the Westgate."

"I'm not interested in them," Barry said. "Tell me about the others."

Jacob screwed up his eyes, picturing the animal wall, and began at the end near Westgate Street. "Pelican, anteater, raccoons, but they're together, so they count as one. Then there's a leopard, a beaver, a vulture, a hyena, and then, I don't know. . . ." He felt guilty, quite unnecessarily he knew, for it was not his fault that the mist and the trees had somehow cloaked that part of the wall. It was not his fault that something had gotten away and escaped into the night.

"Go on!" Barry looked as though his life depended on Jacob's list.

"Apes, mother and baby, but I counted them as one, and a seal, and . . . and a lynx around the corner. I remember that because it's the first animal you see when you pass the clock tower. How many's that?"

"Ten," Barry said.

"That's it, then."

"No, it's not."

"What d'you mean? I counted them, didn't I?"

"You didn't finish, idiot!"

"I did what you wanted," cried Jacob, his face burning. "I went out in the middle of the night, if you want to know, and a policeman caught me and made me go home. He did!"

"The bear and the lioness. You didn't see them," said Barry contemptuously. "I might have known. . . ."

"If you knew they were there, why did you ask me to count them?" exploded Jacob. "I'm not Noah! I told you, a policeman came before I'd finished."

"Calm down. People are looking," Barry muttered through clenched teeth.

"What's so important about it, anyway?" Jacob refused to lower his voice. He was getting into one of those moods where he badly wanted to hit something, but he couldn't do that to Barry, who was small and not very strong. Also, he wanted Barry's help. "You are going to help with my project, aren't you? I did try, Barry."

"What are you two arguing about?" Glyn Daniels sidled up, a nosy parker if ever there was one.

"The animals on the castle wall," Jacob told him, "and how many there are, like."

"Fifteen," Glyn said loftily. "Everyone knows that." He wandered off to poke his nose in somewhere else.

"Fifteen?" repeated Jacob doubtfully. "But I . . :"

"You messed up," said Barry.

"Aren't you going to help me, then?" Jacob asked.

He looked so forlorn and hopeless, Barry sighed and said, "Come on. Let's go into the library before the bell rings."

As they made their way to the library, Barry said, "Don't you know any old people who were in the war? They're the ones to ask."

"Nah," Jacob replied. "My uncle's dad was in the Polish cavalry, but he died when Uncle Tadeusz was only five."

"Cavalry?" Barry stopped dead. "There wasn't any cavalry. Not in that war!"

"There was in Poland," Jacob told him.

"Talk to him, man," Barry said excitedly. "I'll help you to start, but I bet your uncle can tell you some really good stuff. Unique. I mean, who else has a relation in the Polish cavalry? Imagine! Horses against tanks. It's crazy."

Jacob wouldn't have known. It had not occurred to him before that Uncle Tadeusz was special or unusual. He certainly didn't look it. Jacob felt a surge of confidence as Barry pulled a large book from the library shelf and laid it on a table in front of them. When the bell rang ten minutes later, they had made a very promising start.

Back in class, Jacob couldn't concentrate. Animals slipped through his mind. They leaped, ran, flew, and climbed; apes glimpsed through a frieze of branches, pelicans fishing, a vulture feeding on a carcass, and leopards in a jungle, their eyes like green lamps. Why had they suddenly loomed so large in Jacob's life? Why was Barry so fiercely interested in them? He had been kind and helpful with Jacob's project but had refused to talk about the animal wall again.

Jacob's fingers tapped and twisted in his palms until his hands were hot and sweaty. Fifteen, Glyn Daniels had said, and he was the sort who was always right. If Jacob added to his list of ten the two lions at the Westgate, it came to twelve. Add the bear and the lioness, fourteen. So what was missing? He thought of the creature that had slipped from the wall. What was it?

When the last bell rang, Jacob caught Barry's shoulder as he disappeared into the cloakroom. "You can come back to my aunt's place, if you like," he said, "and see the animals for yourself."

Barry was tempted. Jacob could tell by the quick flicker in his eyes, the hesitation before he said, "Nah!"

"Thanks for helping, anyway."

"Yeah. It's okay."

"Dinah Jones wasn't in school!"

Barry shifted his weight from foot to foot, his back-pack dangling like a pendulum. "So what?"

"Well, I need to talk to her."

"About what?" Barry stopped moving.

Jacob felt like saying, "Mind your own business," but asked instead, "Where does she live, then?"

"Anglesey Road, number seventeen," Barry said rather reluctantly. "But she's written *Griffin's Castle* on a board and hung it over the gate."

"Why?"

"Because of the stone griffin. She found it in the garden, all broken, like."

"It's not a castle, is it?"

"'Course not. It's just a big house, empty and a bit spooky. I've got to go. Hey, could you . . . I mean, if you're near the castle and it's dark, could you just check on the bear and the lioness? . . . See if they're still . . . where they should be?"

"Why?" Jacob tried not to sound suspicious. "People can't steal stuff like that. They'd be seen. And there's always a policeman about in that area."

"Oh, never mind," Barry said irritably.

Jacob wanted to mention the quick gray creature that had crept out of the mist, but before he could think how to, Barry was darting through a crowd of boys in his funny, rabbity, leave-me-alone manner. So Jacob left him alone and decided to take the long way back to Auntie Mair's, via Anglesey Road.

The wind had dropped, and the air had a damp, dusky feel. Behind Jacob, children ran to catch buses or wander home. Their chatter and footsteps rose and fell between sudden surges of traffic.

On Anglesey Road, the sounds were so remote, they might have come from another world. The trees here were very tall, and the street was badly lit. There were piles of rubble in some of the gardens. Two of the houses had now been completely demolished, and a Dumpster stood halfway down the road. It was over-flowing with broken furniture, mattresses, and bulging plastic bags. A cat crouched in the Dumpster's giant shadow. Jacob could just make out its rounded shape and long, full tail. As he drew closer, he couldn't help staring at it. The cat gave a low, tremulous mew.

Jacob liked cats. Perhaps this was a stray, and no one would miss it if he took it back to Auntie Mair's. He squatted on the pavement and extended his hand. The cat moaned softly and walked into the light.

"Ugh! What a mess!" Jacob exclaimed, immediately withdrawing his hand. The cat's ear was torn. There was a line of congealed blood over one eye, and patches of flesh could be seen through a shabby coat.

The creature stopped, almost apologetically, and sat at the edge of the curb.

Jacob stood up. "Sorry, cat," he said. "There's no way I could take you anywhere." He walked on, peering at the numbers on gates and pillars, aware that the cat was following.

He would have missed number seventeen, the light was so bad, but he couldn't fail to notice the griffin, perched on a pillar beside the gate. It had been cemented there, very recently, for there was an untidy splotch at the base of the little statue and a strip across its neck.

Jacob stared at the painted sign hanging on the gate. GRIFFIN'S CASTLE. It seemed weird, like a place that was part of a game, a treasure hunt, not a house where someone lived. At the far end of a shadowy garden, a building grew out of scrubby vegetation. Jacob could see that it had once been very grand, but none of its splendor remained. A broken gutter spewed green slime down the wall; the windows were grimy, their frames gray and rotting. The pediments were cracked, and shingles were missing from the roof. It was a dying house.

Except for Jacob, pacing before the gate, the road was quite deserted. And then a woman came walking toward him. Under her winter coat she wore a brightly colored sari, and she was pushing a small stroller. A little boy ran beside her, one hand clutching the arm of the stroller.

The woman smiled as she approached Jacob. "Are you waiting for someone?" she asked as she opened the gate to Griffin's Castle.

"No. I mean . . ." Jacob didn't know what to say. "Does Dinah Jones live in there?" he managed at last, nodding at the tall house.

"Yes. D'you want me to call her for you?"

"No. I'll just wait," Jacob said. But perhaps Dinah would not come out again that night. He didn't really know why he had come, hadn't worked out what he was going to say to Dinah. Something had led him here.

The small boy tripped over something just inside the gate, and the woman gave an exclamation of annoyance. She lifted up a bottle of milk. "They won't come to the door anymore," she told Jacob. "None of them. Not even the postman. They just leave the stuff here.

See!" She showed him a rough wooden box with *Griffin's Castle* scratched on the lid. "Dinah made it."

"But why won't people come to the door?"

She shrugged, but the boy squashed his face against the palings of the gate and, peering up at Jacob, whispered, "Ghosts!"

"Don't be silly, Yusuf," his mother said, and then to Jacob, "He's not so silly, really. There is something. It's the trees perhaps. They're so thick, aren't they? And tall. There's no light and sometimes, I think, no air in this garden."

"House looks a bit ropey, too," Jacob remarked.

"It is," the woman agreed. "It's falling down. We're in the basement, and there are cracks in the ceiling. Soon the roof will tumble right through the house. The floors are all rotten. But we'll be gone before that happens, won't we, Yusuf?"

The boy nodded solemnly and said, "To Canada."

"That's great," Jacob said, "but what about Dinah?"

"Dinah?" The woman looked toward the house. "I

don't know. I'm very sorry for Dinah. I haven't told her yet. Nothing is certain, and we don't want to make her sad for nothing, do we? She's a very special girl."

The baby in the stroller began to whimper, and the woman bent to stroke its face. "I must feed my little one. Are you sure you don't want me to call Dinah?"

"I'll just wait," said Jacob.

He watched them walk through the gloomy garden, keeping to the narrow path as though they were on a tightrope and might plunge into nowhere if they put a foot wrong. By the time the little family had vanished down the basement steps, it was quite dark.

A light came on at the top of the building, and a figure moved into the window. She stood silhouetted against the light, utterly still. Jacob could feel the force of her gaze and something else, a stirring in the trees that seemed almost to come in answer to the silent call from the watcher in the window.

Dew settled on the ground and froze in glistening strands. Vapor swirled about the trees, and a creature stepped quietly onto the path. At first Jacob thought it was a cat, but no cat was so huge. It sniffed the frost for a moment and then looked toward the gate. And as Jacob stood, too petrified to move, another creature appeared and began to walk toward him. And then he knew what had slipped through the mist around the animal wall. A wolf!

With his eyes on the wolf, Jacob moved away from the gate. He told himself that when he reached the spruce that overhung the pavement, he would hide behind its branches and observe. Feeling his way with the tips of his fingers on the wall, he stepped backward very slowly. But he never reached the tree. His hand made contact with something soft, and when he turned to see what he had touched, Jacob came face-to-face with a bear. His hand lay over the bear's paw.

Jacob's scream hit his ears from a great distance. His own voice could hardly penetrate the wall of terror that rose around him. He ran, leaped, and slipped down endless Anglesey Road. He raced through streams of traffic, getting closer to the safe city, his bookbag thumping his back at every bound. By the time he reached the castle, the stitch in his side ached like a knife wound, and the cold air filling his lungs felt as heavy as lead.

He crossed the road away from the animal wall, turning his back on the place where he now knew the bear, the wolf, and the lioness should be. He did not want to know, he told himself; he could not bear to know that they were gone. "They're stone," he said aloud. "They *can't* be in Dinah's garden." But just before he turned down Westgate Street, he glanced back. The pelican, raccoons, leopard, beaver, vulture, and hyena all registered quickly in his brain, but then the wall seemed to disappear into a tunnel of black shadows beneath the trees. *He could not see the wolf, the bear, or the lioness!*

Why hadn't Barry warned him? Why hadn't he told the truth?

Jacob tore down Westgate Street, and when he

stumbled through his aunt's front door, he was already calling, "Uncle Tad, tell me about your father and the war!" Jacob wanted to question, gossip, argue about anything except the animal wall. He wanted Uncle Tad to talk the night away so he could forget the creatures in the garden of Griffin's Castle. Because they could not be real, could they? *Could they?*

Over tea, Uncle Tadeusz told Jacob all he knew about the Pomorska cavalry charge of 1939. He told it so well that Jacob could smell leather and horses and gunpowder. He could hear the creak and ring of saddles and harnesses and the drum of a thousand hooves accelerating, pounding the earth before the grim, gray, terrible tanks. And he could see the fierce, proud, brave faces, charging at death. And it almost worked. The images that Uncle Tadeusz conjured up almost buried Dinah's ghostly creatures so deep that Jacob believed they couldn't haunt him. But it was not enough.

After tea Jacob fetched his notebook and made his

uncle repeat every word so that he could write it down because Auntie Mair would never allow reading or writing during meals. But it was partly to bury, even deeper, the glinting black eyes of a bear that he had touched, a bear who couldn't really be there.

When Jacob had written as much as he could and his uncle had checked the work for spelling, they went into the living room. But his uncle did not turn on the television as he usually did. He sat beside Jacob on the sofa and asked, "What is it, Jacob? Something has happened. You're trying to listen to me, trying hard, but your heart isn't in it."

Jacob folded his arms tight across his chest. He couldn't think of a way to begin. He stared at the television, hoping that it would just pop on and save him from talking.

"Come on, Jake." His uncle nudged him affectionately.

And Jacob thought, *If anyone can understand this, it's a man whose father thought he could defeat a row of tanks with his sword.* So he said, "There's a girl at school called Dinah Jones. She's very clever. She can do practically anything. She lives in this old house that's falling down. . . ." He could not continue.

The only light in the room came from the flickering gas fire. It played on Uncle Tadeusz's patient face, and Jacob imagined him to be a weary Polish cavalryman, sitting by his campfire in the dawn of that terrible day in 1939.

He tried another tactic. "There are kids at school," he said, "who have had a tough time. Sometimes you can tell because they act kind of crazy, but the others, you never know unless they talk about it, and then it surprises you because they seem so normal. They don't actually talk to me, you know. I just listen."

Auntie Mair walked in and switched on a lamp. "Why are you two sitting in the dark?" she asked.

"Shh! Jacob's telling me something," Uncle Tadeusz said.

Auntie Mair settled herself in her favorite chair and put on her reading glasses.

And then it came to Jacob in a message of startling clarity. He saw what had happened, and even what might happen next.

"Dinah Jones is different." He spoke fast and urgently, before the truth could escape him. "She's seen things, been in places that are horrible. But she'll never, never tell. They've got right into her, like, right deep into her, and she can't get away. And the animals are the same. They can't talk about what it's like to be hunted and chained and to have your claws and your teeth pulled out or to starve very slowly. So she's invited them into her garden, where they'll be together. Safety in numbers. But Griffin's Castle is falling down. And supposing *all* the animals come. Maybe she'll never get out again."

"Jacob." His aunt leaned forward and looked earnestly into his face. "Do you want us to do something for this girl?"

"I don't think you can," Jacob said. "She's got a mother."

"But these animals, Jake boy?" his uncle asked. "Where do they come from?"

"The wall," Jacob told him. "The animal wall." And in answer to his uncle's puzzled frown, he went on. "Perhaps a desperate person, like Dinah, can make things happen. Things that could never normally happen in real life, I mean. D'you think that's possible?"

A look of thoughtful surprise passed across his uncle's face. "Perhaps," he said, "when my father and his comrades charged into a storm of tank fire, they died believing they could win the war." He smiled and added, "Who knows what is possible, Jacob?"

ATTACK!

Gomer didn't come near Griffin's Castle for a week. Even the milkman and the postman wouldn't come to the door. Dinah was sorry for this because Tahira complained of having to fetch the milk in her slippers.

There were three animals now. The wolf had been there every night since the first of December and the full moon, the night he had led Dinah away from the graveyard and back to Griffin's Castle. Today it was the sixth, and a funny chip of a moon still hung in the sky when Dinah walked to school.

The other children could talk of nothing but Christmas: their trees, their gifts, the food they would have, the nuts and chocolate stuffed in their stockings. The playground and the classrooms rang with the tinselly sound of Christmas. And Dinah was swept along with it. She made cards to hand out. She helped to decorate the classroom, hung a cardboard reindeer on the school tree, spread glitter on the windows, and sang carols.

No one on Anglesey Road made much of an effort. Someone hung colored lights in a window three doors away from Griffin's Castle, and there was a wreath on a gate at the end of the road. But otherwise Christmas wasn't happening there.

Dinah cleaned milk bottle tops and cut them into stars. She painted strips of newspaper and made a chain that went all the way around the empty Harp Room. Rosalie said it would be a waste to buy decorations. On Saturday she took Dinah down into the city. They stayed until the shops closed and gazed at the strands of Christmas lights twinkling above the crowds.

Gomer had given Rosalie a bonus, and she was waving ten-pound notes about as though she'd won the lottery. She gave two to Dinah and told her to buy something she really wanted. Dinah didn't know until she saw the animals. They were standing in a row in a craft-shop window, small carved creatures with painted eyes and feet. Dinah dragged her mother inside, and while Rosalie tried on embroidered slippers and silk shirts, Dinah carefully plucked a wolf from the window. They only had a polar bear, but she picked that out, too. The male lion wouldn't do, however. Dinah searched the shop.

"Can I help?" asked a girl who didn't look much older than Dinah.

"I'm looking for a lioness!"

The girl smiled and pulled a long tray from a shelf behind her. Dinah couldn't believe her luck. Surrounded by tiny bells and carved boxes stood a small bronze lioness. Beside her sat a dragon.

"That's it," said Dinah. "And I'll take the dragon, too."

Tahira had explained that her family didn't celebrate

Christmas, but Dinah bought the dragon for Yusuf, as a sort of talisman, to keep him safe. Before she left the shop, she bought a rattle, carved like a birdcage, for the baby.

Rosalie found scarves for Gran and Auntie June and a book for Granddad. Dinah picked out identical bead necklaces for Angela and Julie, so they wouldn't argue. She would not have chosen them for herself, but she thought she knew exactly what June's girls would like.

Rosalie didn't mention a present for Gomer. Dinah imagined it would be something very special, something that would cost more than her mother could afford.

When they had finished shopping, they sat in the window of a café and watched the lights glittering in the trees. It was such a good day, better even than the few hours they had snatched on a beach in the summer. And then Dinah had to ask about Christmas, and everything went wrong again.

"Will Gomer come?" she asked. "And will we eat a

turkey in our kitchen? Afterward we could light a fire in the Harp Room, and we can have a tree in there. . . ." She kept talking because her mother's face had taken on an awkward, guilty look, and Dinah dreaded what she might say.

"Look," Rosalie said at last. "You mustn't get too . . . You mustn't make plans yet, Di. Gomer hasn't decided."

Dinah plowed on. "I think we should ask Mrs. Gwynne to share our Christmas. She'd love to be back in her own home. She can still play the harp, you know. Arthritis hasn't struck her yet. She's got lovely hands."

"Dinah!" her mother said savagely. "There isn't a harp!"

"There is," Dinah shouted, repeating in a whisper, "There is! There is! And there's a bear and a wolf and a lioness in the garden. You can't see them because you're growing old, and because you're so blind with passion for Gomer Gwynne, you can't see beyond the end of your nose!" Dinah sank back, pleased and exhausted.

Rosalie's eyes glittered dangerously. "Get up," she said. "We're going!"

"I haven't finished my muffin," Dinah complained.

"You won't get away with the things you've just said, Dinah Jones!" Her mother stood and pushed her chair back. Sweeping up her pile of shopping, she walked off between the tables in long, bad-tempered strides.

Dinah followed meekly, wishing she hadn't spoiled their happy day.

They didn't speak to each other on the bus or on the long walk up Anglesey Road. But when they reached the gate of Griffin's Castle, Rosalie said, "Dinah, why did you have to put all this rubbish out here!"

"The griffin belongs there," Dinah said, "and a sign makes it look more permanent."

"But it *isn't* permanent!"

"It could be," Dinah said under her breath.

Rosalie sighed irritably and pushed open the gate. "It's getting me down. That's the truth," she said as she led the way up the path. "Sometimes I feel I can't breathe. It's these trees. I can't say I blame the milk-man, dumping his bottles back there."

Dinah peered into the gloom beneath the sweeping branches. They should have been there. She needed the comfort of their glowing eyes and strong shining bodies. But she couldn't see them. A wave of panic swept over her. "I can't live without you!" she murmured.

She was answered by a soft growl from the shadows near the steps.

Rosalie stopped dead and dropped a bag. "God, what was that?" she yelped.

Dinah smiled. "A cat. It won't hurt you."

"Sometimes I think there are beasts in those trees." Rosalie's voice was quavery and fretful.

"There are," Dinah told her cheerfully.

Her mother almost ran up the steps. She unlocked the door with nervous, twitching fingers.

The musty smell inside the house was stronger than ever. The heaters seemed to have made it worse.

Warmth drew countless unseen fungi from the walls. Moldy parasites crept across the floorboards, reeking silently, pressing close against the doors and fingering Rosalie's new curtains.

They would be banished at Christmas. Dinah took a peek into the Harp Room. It was too cold for smells in there. And on Christmas Day the glory of a glittering tree would blind anything horrible that tried to get too close.

"Di, come out of there. It's freezing," Rosalie called.

"I was just thinking about the tree," said Dinah. She took her shopping upstairs to examine it again. Where would she put the bronze lioness, she wondered, beside her bed or under the pillow? But when she got to her room, the real animals drew her to the window. She pushed it open and peered over the sill.

The wolf was sitting on the path right below her, and when he looked up, Dinah was immediately struck by his penetrating gaze. The other animals were busy. The lioness was eating something close to the trees.

The bear stood tall as he rubbed his back against the griffin's pillar.

"You're all invited to a Christmas feast," Dinah called. "Plenty of meat, or insects and vegetables if you prefer, good company, and party poppers filled with wishes that come true."

The lioness left her prey and walked closer to the house. The bear dropped on all fours and moved behind the wolf. All three animals looked up at Dinah, and such a haunting, savage light was beamed on her, she had to step back, almost breathless.

A car drew up, and Gomer Gwynne got out.

Dinah watched him. He stood at the gate for at least a minute before entering the garden. She couldn't see what he was doing because he was beyond the reach of the light thrown out by the windows.

The animals turned to Gomer. A row of three, they straddled the path. He would have to walk around them. Dinah heard a cracking sound, and then Gomer walked into the light, carrying the sign she had tied to the gate. He had split the wood in half.

He walked confidently until he reached the row of animals, and then he stopped, confused and angry. He swore and ran one hand through his hair.

Did he see them? Could he sense their wildness, smell cruelty, or feel violence in the air? Man and beasts were motionless. Then Gomer lifted the broken sign across his chest.

"It's madness," he muttered.

Three ragged sounds tore through the air. And Gomer, swearing endlessly, raced out toward the trees, then back, giving the animals as wide a berth as possible.

Dinah could not see if he reached the steps, but she heard the front door slam and shouting in the hall.

She crept downstairs and listened for a moment at the kitchen door.

"I'm not a superstitious man," Gomer declared,

"but, Rosie, this house is trying to tell me something. There's a . . . a presence out there, evil, ghastly. I can't believe I'm saying this. It sounds ridiculous."

"No, Gomer," said Rosalie. "I've felt it."

"I don't believe in ghosts, Rosalie!"

"Nor me."

"Dinah doesn't muck about with Ouija boards, does she, meddle in the occult, that sort of thing?"

"Gomer, of course not," Rosalie protested.

"I'm sorry, Rosie, but she's not like a child. There's something going on in her head all the time. They say that extraordinary children can wake things up . . . poltergeists et cetera . . . and she's never liked me."

"There are no poltergeists here"— Rosalie sighed — "just damp and rotten floors."

"I'll find somewhere for you soon," Gomer said, his voice sounding calmer. "I must have been mad to put you here, but it seemed the best solution. I'm selfish, Rosalie! I wanted to get you closer. Swansea was too far away."

"I know. We've seen worse, Di and me. We keep losing our place on the list for rehousing. I'm too impatient, see!"

"I swear I thought the floors were sound."

"Dry rot," said Rosalie. "It stinks, too!"

"Come away with me for Christmas."

"I want to, Gomer, but . . ."

"What about Dinah?" Gomer said angrily.

Dinah ambled into the room. "Talking about me?" she said.

"What d'you want for Christmas, Dinah?" Gomer asked. She could see the effort it cost him. "Make a list, and I'll see what I can do."

You can't buy me off, that's for sure, thought Dinah. "I want a log fire, a beautiful tree, and a happy family." She flashed a grim smile at both of them, sat down, and poured herself a mug of tea.

Rosalie glanced at Gomer, but he kept his metal-gray eyes fixed on Dinah. "Happy families are hard to come by, Dinah," he said, "these days, anyway. Count your blessings, girl. You've got a wonderful mom who needs a break. So make your list, and if it's clothes or music or a T.V. of your own, I'll do my best. But you'll have to get your log fire and your Christmas tree from someone else."

"I see!" Dinah looked down into her tea. She hated the anguished, guilty look her mother wore.

"And while we're about it"— Gomer stood up and grabbed the broken sign from the dresser —"I don't want you mucking up my property. No more signs on the gate, right?"

"A house has got to have a name," Dinah murmured.

"A number is good enough," he told her, his voice harsh with irritation. "And I want that monster taken off the wall."

"It's a griffin," Dinah protested, "and it belongs here. It's part of your family history. You should be proud of it."

Gomer gave an exasperated groan, and Rosalie,

clasping Dinah's hand, said, "The house doesn't belong to us, love. Please do as Gomer asks."

"All right," Dinah said sullenly. "But I fixed the griffin with cement. I got it from the builders down the road, just a bit in a plastic bag. I'll have to get a friend to help me bash it off. D'you think your mom would like it?"

Gomer smiled as though his teeth ached. "No," he said.

Rosalie changed the subject quickly. "Gomer's taking me out to lunch tomorrow, Di. You'll be all right, won't you?"

"Great," said Dinah. "I've got a passion for baked beans."

"Don't be like that, Di. There's cold chicken in the fridge. And frozen french fries. You can heat them in the oven."

Gomer was already leaving by the front door. Rosalie went out with him. Dinah knew that they would walk together as far as the gate, so she couldn't call the animals. She didn't want to break the uneasy truce with Rosalie.

She decided to visit the Harp Room to arrange the furniture and choose a place for the Christmas tree. There was a spruce sapling in the garden, only three feet high. She could dig it out and hang her silver bottle tops on it. She would ask Jacob or Barry to help her move the griffin mirror and place it above the fireplace. And then she would set candles in saucers along the mantelpiece. Reflected candlelight would fill the room with stars.

Dinah stood in the Harp Room with her back to the door, her confidence returning. She would not go to Gran's. Never, never again. Christmas was already on its way to her here, in a real family room. Tahira and her family would come, even if they didn't celebrate Christmas. Yusuf could unwrap his dragon beside the fire. He would be so surprised and pleased.

In her mind Dinah placed the little boy on a bright

cushion and the baby lying in the armchair from Rosalie's room. Mrs. Gwynne would have the best chair from the kitchen; she would draw it up to the harp and play for them. Her music would be in a minor key, timeless and beautiful, and the animals would come closer and listen, slightly puzzled, to the sound of a distant, singing waterfall.

A disturbance in the garden broke into Dinah's dream, and she ran to the window. Rosalie and Gomer stood on the pavement, arranging their Christmas without her, no doubt. A cat had sneaked through the open gate, the same scruffy animal that had led her to the graveyard. It was trying to creep closer to the house, but the wild beasts would not let it. Their coats burned fiercely, and they paced in a line across the path and up to the trees, not allowing the cat an inch of safe ground to dash through. The lioness's tail swung furiously. And then the cat arched itself like a spring, stepped sideways, and spit at her.

All three animals froze, and Dinah, quite without thinking, gave a little cheer of admiration. But all at once the enraged lioness leaped forward.

The cat screamed and tore out of the garden. Had the lioness injured it? Dinah wondered. *Whose side are you on?* she asked herself.

Gomer's car slid away, and Rosalie returned to the house. She held her arms across her body. For warmth or comfort? She didn't see the creatures, but Dinah watched her mother flinch when she passed them, as though a cold draft had suddenly struck her shoulders.

When Dinah went into the kitchen, Rosalie was hunched over the table. Her face was pinched and miserable. Dinah would have done anything to make her smile.

"I don't mind about tomorrow," she said brightly. "I've got homework and stuff to do. And anyway I like being on my own."

Her mother threw her a grateful smile, but the pinched look did not really leave her face.

Dinah had been waiting to tell her mother about the grave, but she wanted it to be a special moment, when she would have Rosalie's full attention. Perhaps now was the time.

"I found my great-grandmother's grave," she said. "The headstone is beautiful. D'you want me to take you there?"

"Your gran took us," Rosalie said. "I remember this great lump of granite that your great-grandfather had dragged all the way from the mountains. And he insisted on adding Welsh to the inscription. I was scared. I don't like cemeteries. We didn't go again." She picked up a newspaper and scanned the headlines.

Dinah realized she had misjudged her moment. Rosalie was being torn apart again, only this time it was between Dinah and Gomer, not Gran.

"I don't want to be a millstone," Dinah murmured.

"What?" Rosalie looked up, frowning.

"Nothing," Dinah said.

Dinah went up to her room and stood at the window, looking down on the animals.

They responded slowly this time, first the wolf, then the bear. But for a few minutes the lioness kept her back to Dinah, and when she finally turned to face the window, she looked sullen and resentful, almost as if she had heard Dinah cheer for the cat and could not forgive it.

"I didn't mean it," Dinah told the lioness. "But he was brave. He knew you could crunch him to death."

She must have slept long and deeply. Her mother had already left when she went down to the kitchen for breakfast.

There was a note on the table, reminding her about the cold chicken and the frozen french fries.

Dinah took a chair and a slice of toast into the Harp Room. She drew her chair close to the window and sat down to look at the trees, each one frosted in a different way. A pale sun lit the cobwebs encircling the trees like strands of diamonds. Seventeen Christmas trees Dinah counted, not including the sapling. She must remember to ask Barry about a spade.

An unfamiliar car drew up outside the gate. It was bright red and a back hubcap was missing. To Dinah's surprise, the man who emerged from the car came straight through the gate and walked up the path. He was smiling to himself, as if he had won a prize or had hidden treasures in the four or five fancy bags he carried.

There was a shout from the basement steps, and Yusuf sped across the garden and hurled himself at the man, who dropped the bags and lifted the little boy into the air.

"Karim!" Dinah murmured.

She could hear Yusuf's screams of joy above the man's deep laughter.

Dinah pulled her chair away from the window and went back to the kitchen. Tahira's family moved through the rooms below, gossiping, laughing, and singing.

Dinah heard the clatter of saucepans and dishes and sat almost transfixed by their busy happiness. A strong spicy smell reached her, mysterious and delicious. They must be having a party, something special to celebrate Karim's return.

The bell rang, but Dinah didn't hear it until someone rapped on the front door. Outside, she found Tahira dressed in glittering red and gold.

"Oh!" said Dinah, taken aback by her friend's sudden splendor. "You look so . . . so fabulous, Tahira!"

"Are you alone, Dinah?" Tahira asked.

"Yes," she admitted.

"Come and have some food with us. My husband has come home."

"Has he?" Dinah said shyly. She could not admit that she had seen his happy arrival.

"Will you come?" Tahira looked genuinely welcoming.

Dinah was about to accept when she was assailed by a wonderful scene: a party in the empty Harp Room.

"Come up here," she exclaimed. "Bring everything. The sun's bursting into our rooms, and it's so dark downstairs."

"D'you think . . . ?" Tahira looked uncertain.

"They won't be back for ages," Dinah assured her. "They're out for the day. Come on!"

"Okay." Tahira almost giggled with pleasure. "It would be really nice. I'll be back in half an hour."

"The door will be open," Dinah told her, "to let the sun in." And warm the heart of Griffin's Castle, she nearly added. She was going to be very busy. First, she pushed the kitchen table into the Harp Room, put a chair on the table, and climbed up on it, carefully lifting a bowl of soapy water with her. She washed the crystals of the chandelier, or as many as she could reach, and then climbed down. The sun made the glass sparkle with the strength of a hundred tiny candles.

She had just set four places around the table when Tahira and Karim walked in, carrying trays of food: joints of chicken, two kinds of rice, thick creamy sauces, and vegetables that Dinah had never seen, all in bowls of different colors. The room was filled with so many strong and exotic aromas that it seemed like a place in another country.

When Karim saw the grand marble fireplace and the empty grate, he raised his eyebrows and smiled thoughtfully. Dinah felt that he had read her mind.

"We must have a fire," he declared.

Tahira looked apprehensive, but Karim refused to listen to the list of pitfalls they might encounter: the bats' and birds' nests that might block the flue, the soot that might fill the room, the chimney that could crumble, and the fire that might burn the house down.

"It's cold in here," Karim argued. "We shall have a fire, Tahira, if only for the baby." And he was gone.

Dinah was delighted with him. *If Karim stays here,* she thought, *then everything will be all right.*

In twenty minutes Karim was back with a bag of smokeless fuel and fire lighters. The chimney didn't smoke. The frosty air drew the flames upward, and the fire glowed fiercely. It was as though Karim's optimism had banished all of the threatening incidents that his wife had foreseen.

Dinah sat with her back to the long windows. The chandelier glittered above her, and the fire blazed before her. The baby slept in Rosalie's armchair, just as Dinah had imagined she would. Karim and Tahira talked about the place where they'd been born; they told Dinah about the names of the trees, the colors of the plants, the monkeys, and the snakes. But Dinah never told them about her past; it was behind her now, forgotten, buried. When Karim talked about a tiger that he had seen, Dinah was tempted to mention the lioness in the garden, but Yusuf, already frightened by Karim's tiger, was watching her intently, expecting the worst. He knew there was a creature in the trees, but he hated to talk about it.

So Dinah kept quiet for a while, and then suddenly found herself saying, "This is the best day of my life!"

Her friends looked at one another and then at Dinah,

and then Karim said quietly, "Good. That's good, Dinah, but there will be many even better days for you, I know."

"Yes," Dinah said. "Christmas!"

Tahira smiled awkwardly, as if she knew something that Dinah didn't. "Of course, Christmas!" she said.

The sun dipped below the horizon, and the embers in the grate softened to a radiant crimson. A shadowy dusk filled the garden, and a second frost sharpened the ground where the sunlight had not reached. Soon the animals would arrive.

They began to clear the table and did not hear a car draw up or see two figures walk toward the house. But Dinah heard the front door open, and her heart began to pound.

Gomer did not hesitate. He must have seen them through the window. Quick, angry strides brought him bursting into the room. "What's going on here?" he demanded.

Karim, not at all perturbed, replied, "We're warming the house up for you, Mr. Gwynne."

"You're trespassing, and the whole place stinks. Put that fire out before the chimney catches," Gomer ranted.

"Don't speak to me like that, Mr. Gwynne," Karim said quietly. "Your basement is a disgrace, and this place isn't much better. The children were freezing."

"You were glad enough to take it." Gomer strode farther into the room and glared at Dinah. "I suppose you're responsible for this."

Rosalie appeared behind Gomer. Dinah hoped that she would say something.

"Don't take it out on Dinah," Karim warned. "You promised to put in better heating and a decent stove. You said you'd get the electricity put right. You took advantage, Mr. Gwynne. You broke an agreement because I wasn't here. That's not right. It's dishonest."

Gomer put his hands on the table. His cold eyes rested on Karim. "If you don't like it, Mr. Malik," he said, soft as a serpent, "you can get out."

Dinah couldn't bear any more. "You can't!" she cried, but Karim caught her hand and hushed her.

"We're going, Mr. Gwynne," he said with satisfaction. "Don't worry. We'll be out on Thursday. We're going to Canada. It's all arranged."

Dinah stared at Tahira, who couldn't meet her gaze.

"The sooner, the better," Gomer shouted. "Now clean up this mess." He swept out, pushing Rosalie before him, and slammed the door.

"You never said," murmured Dinah, staring at them. "To Canada. It's so far."

"I'm sorry, Dinah." Tahira touched her arm. "Nothing was certain. Karim has only just . . ."

"You should have told me," Dinah blazed.

She rushed out and up the stairs, stumbling in her haste to get away, bounding two steps at a time, so angry she wanted to kick right through the treads. Pushing her door open, she ran straight to the window and flung it wide.

It was still not quite dark.

They must come before Gomer left. Everything was his fault. Dinah was certain the Maliks would have stayed if he'd done the things he'd promised. He was stealing Rosalie away, letting the house fall down. He had to be punished properly this time.

Looking down, she saw Tahira and Karim carrying the remains of their splendid party down into the basement. Gomer had obviously locked the door in the hall. She wanted to call out, but there was a gulf between them now, deeper than the long walls of the house, and Gomer had made it.

An icy dusk crept past Dinah and filled her room. The trees shivered beneath a brittle frost. Dinah felt the cold invading her body, numbing her arms, her face and fingers.

"Come on," she whispered urgently.

The twilight faded, and night smothered the garden. A dark and deadly night, unrelieved by the smallest patch of light. And then they came.

First the lioness, her gleaming teeth bared, and then

the bear, tossing his head, his body heavy with suppressed fury that Dinah could almost feel. The wolf came last, cautious and purposeful, as though he were on a spring that only needed the slightest touch to catapult him at someone's throat.

And in the dark they brought their own light, for there was no other source. They patrolled the path, waiting, with Dinah.

The front door opened, and Gomer ran down the steps, eager to be gone. He had not taken more than a few paces before they were on him. It was a swift and silent execution.

The animals looked up for Dinah's approval.

"Excellent," she said.

She went downstairs, deliberately taking her time. Rosalie was in the kitchen, still in her coat.

"Gomer's lying in the garden," Dinah told her. "I think he's dead!"

MEETING THE
ANIMALS

"Have you got a spade?" Dinah asked Barry. They were filing into class after the first break.

"A spade," Barry repeated. "You mean for digging?"

"Of course for digging," Dinah said.

"What d'you want it for? To bury a body?" He giggled nervously.

Dinah sighed. "I suppose it's too much to hope for. I suppose you've got a garden the size of a hanky and a dad who can't dig."

"As a matter of fact, we grow vegetables," Barry said huffily. "I'll bring the spade tonight if you like."

"Thanks." Dinah wandered over to her desk.

Barry thought she looked a bit peculiar. Restless,

electric. The word *explosive* came to mind. Yes, that was it. Dinah was keeping her lid on, but only just. Any moment now she might explode.

There was someone else in class who looked explosive. Jacob Rose had been staring at Barry all morning. Luckily, Mrs. Price had called him back just before break so Barry had escaped in a crowd. He managed to stay hidden when Jacob finally came out, but he realized he couldn't avoid him all day. He was caught as he tried to dodge into the cafeteria at lunchtime.

"I want to talk to you!" Jacob grabbed Barry by the back of his sweater.

"Get off!" squealed Barry, trying to catch the lunchroom monitor's eye.

The monitor pretended not to notice and hurried by.

Jacob hauled Barry into the corridor and pinned him against the wall. "Why didn't you tell me?" he demanded.

"Tell you what?" Barry squirmed against Jacob's strong right arm.

"About the animals!" Jacob hissed in Barry's face.

"What about them?"

"You know! I went to Dinah's place on Friday night, Griffin's Castle, and they were there. I could have died of fright. Why didn't you tell me? I know it was them, the ones from the wall, because they were the ones you asked about, the bear and the lioness. And now there's a wolf!"

Barry's throat went dry. He stopped wriggling. "You saw them?" he rasped.

"You bet I did." Jacob released his grip.

"Look, I didn't know they'd be there." Barry felt shaken. "Come outside for a minute."

"What about your lunch?" Jacob always brought sandwiches.

"I don't *care* about my lunch. This is important."

"You can have one of my sandwiches," Jacob offered.

"Thanks."

They walked up to the playing field, where there was less chance of being overheard.

"Tell me what happened!" Barry said.

Jacob told him. It poured out in a jumbled rush: the girl at the window, the lioness appearing, the wolf that must have slipped from the wall on the night that Jacob was watching for Barry. And last of all, in a low and dramatic voice, Jacob described the bear.

"You touched it?" Barry cried incredulously.

Jacob gave a slow, vehement nod.

"You never!" Barry shook his head. "Come off it, Jacob! I thought maybe they were spirits or sort of conjured up by Dinah because she's so — well, you know, strange. You can't touch spirits."

"I touched it," Jacob repeated solemnly.

Barry had to believe him. "What are we going to do?" he said.

Jacob looked puzzled.

"Someone should be told."

"No one can do anything," Jacob said. "Except us."

"Why us?" said Barry in alarm. He snatched off his

glasses and rubbed the lenses with a grubby thumb, convinced that seeing better would help him to think.

"We're the only ones who've seen them," Jacob told him.

"But *I* haven't," Barry protested.

Jacob gave what Barry considered a rather condescending smile. "You will, Barry," he said. "I know you will."

The bell rang, and suddenly realizing that neither of them had eaten, Jacob thrust a huge chunk of garlic sausage into Barry's hand. "It's my favorite stuff," he sang out as he sprinted down the path, "but you can have it, Barry."

Barry stared at the sausage in dismay, then thrust it into his pocket.

Art was the first class after lunch. Barry sat beside Dinah. As in every other subject, she excelled, especially when it came to painting. But today she seemed at a loss. She dabbed at her work, washed it out, began again. She chewed her paintbrush, then splashed swaths of color across the paper. The shapes made no sense to Barry until the class was over and he was about to leave the room. Looking back at Dinah's painting, he could see a cat stretched out on the low branch of a tree. Was it a cat? He tilted his head the other way. No, it was a lioness.

"Don't forget the spade," Dinah said in Barry's ear as they walked out of school after the last class.

Barry jumped nervously and said, "I won't."

Kevin always beat him home. He ran. Barry sauntered, not wanting to draw attention to himself. Today he moved exceptionally slowly. A frown of concentration ached across his forehead, and he walked straight into Glyn Daniels and David Watson.

"Watch out, Tiny!" sneered Glyn.

David grabbed Barry's bag and swung it out of reach. "You're blind, aren't you, little midget? See if you can find your bag."

Barry stood still, miserably watching his bag being

dragged through a puddle. "Please," he said in a voice that sounded pathetic even to him. "My books'll get wet."

"Aw, dear!" said the gang of two in mock sympathy.

All at once, and seemingly out of nowhere, Jacob Rose leaped past Barry, wrested the bag from David with one hand and sent him flying with the other.

"Run!" yelled Jacob.

Barry ran. He could hear Glyn and David shouting behind him, but he knew they wouldn't follow. People might tease Jacob, but they never tackled him.

When they had safely turned a corner, Jacob stopped and let Barry catch up with him. He held out the bag.

"You didn't have to do that," Barry said.

"I know I didn't have to."

"Thanks, anyway." Barry took his muddy bag and stared at it ruefully. "It was new," he said.

"Jerks!" declared Jacob. "I could've thumped them both if you'd wanted."

"I didn't want you to," said Barry. "Were you following me?"

"No, I wasn't," Jacob cried. "I go this way, don't I? My mom's at home tonight." He ran off, leaping and shadowboxing, his gangly figure looking as though it had been fitted together incorrectly.

Barry had turned the wrong way when he had followed Jacob. Now he had to retrace his steps, and by the time he got home, both his brothers were halfway through their tea.

"You stink," said Kevin as Barry sat beside him.

Barry glanced reproachfully at Kevin. Everything was going wrong today. Why did he stink? He remembered Jacob's garlic sausage.

"It's probably this," he said, laying the sausage on the table.

"Uuuuuurgh!" His brothers leaned away from the table. Even Mrs. Hughes wrinkled her nose.

"What *is* it, Barry?" she asked.

"Garlic sausage," Barry told her. He knew now why people called Jacob "Smelly Rose." He would have to find a way to warn Jacob about the garlic without offending him. "Jacob Rose gave it to me," he said. "It's his favorite stuff."

"Put it in the trash," said his mother.

While Barry dropped the sausage in the trash can, he asked casually, "Can I take Dad's spade around to Dinah Jones?"

"Whatever for?" asked Mrs. Hughes.

Kevin snorted. "Is she burying a body?"

Barry grinned. "She wouldn't say. But I'll find out, won't I, if I take the spade?"

An hour later Barry was walking down Anglesey Road. He carried his father's spade over his shoulder and sang "Heigh Ho" under his breath. If anyone questioned him, he would say he was going to bury something. It sounded impressive and would surely deter further interrogation. An image of the seven dwarfs sprang to mind and was quickly banished. He was small but not a dwarf.

Barry sang out boldly now. There was no one about

on Anglesey Road. No sound except his own cheerful voice to spur him on down the desolate street.

And then, just before he reached Griffin's Castle, a cat dropped down from a Dumpster standing on the road and ran across Barry's path.

"It's you!" Barry bent and stroked the cat's head. When he set off again, the cat followed, occasionally nudging his leg, then running ahead, almost as though it were trying to hurry him.

Dinah was waiting for him in the garden. She opened the gate with a slight bow. "Well done. You've brought it!" She saw the cat. "Don't let that thing in. It's mangy."

"Poor cat!" Barry closed the gate behind him.

The murky garden had a smothered feel. The trees seemed taller, closer, and there were no lights in the house.

"Is your mom at home?" he asked.

"No, she's gone to see a friend in the hospital."

Dinah's voice had an edge to it. "The man you saw here."

"What's wrong with him?"

"I don't know. Heart failure? He collapsed right here." She pointed to the path. "I thought he was dead."

Barry shuddered. "That stuff I said about burying a body could have been true."

"Yes." She sounded very solemn.

"What've I got to dig, then?"

"This!" She pointed to a small fir tree, a sapling growing in the shadow of its tall parent. A hurricane lamp had been placed close to the little tree. Without it, Barry doubted whether he would have seen it. He thrust the spade into the ground beside the sapling. It penetrated a few inches, no more. Barry stood on the blade. It sank two more inches.

"You'll have to go deeper than that," Dinah told him. "We must get the roots out so I can replant it."

"It's tough earth," Barry explained feebly.

"I'll try." Dinah repeated Barry's actions, then jumped on the blade, without success.

"What're you doing?" a voice called from the wall.

"Oh, no, it's Jacob Rose," Barry groaned.

"So what? He can help," Dinah said tartly. "Come on in," she shouted to Jacob.

Jacob wandered over to them, his hands in his pockets, smiling happily. "Hi! So what's going on?"

"We're trying to dig up this tree," Dinah told him. "But we're not strong enough."

"Roots an' all? Let me try!"

Barry scowled.

Jacob pulled the spade out of the ground and attacked at a different angle, thrusting the blade down with one foot. The spade sank smoothly into the earth.

"Oh, well done!" cried Dinah.

"You probably hit a stone before," Jacob suggested, looking anxiously at Barry. "But it'll take a while if we've got to get all the roots out."

"I'll get a bucket." Dinah flew off across the garden.

"What are you doing here?" muttered Barry when Dinah had disappeared.

"It's a free country!" Jacob's face was in shadow, but Barry could sense the hurt behind Jacob's quick, indignant answer, and he knew the tall boy's cheeks were burning. He stepped away as a clod of earth hit his shoe.

Jacob worked silently for a while, then straightened up and asked, in a hushed voice, "Have you seen them yet?"

"No," Barry said, "and I don't . . ."

As he spoke, the cypress tree behind him rustled, and the spiky foliage on the lower branches trembled violently. Barry leaped away and stood behind Jacob. The taller boy watched the tree for a moment, passed a hand across his mouth, and set to work with the spade again.

Jacob had his back to the trees now. Barry watched the deft movements of the spade in the lamplight. His eye traveled up the little tree, which had begun to shiver as its roots were freed from the earth. And then, behind Jacob, Barry saw the bear.

He wanted to yell to Jacob, but he couldn't. He froze to his patch of earth, his mouth dropping open.

"What is it?" Jacob looked up. Barry didn't have to tell him. Jacob could feel the strange compression in the air; he could smell the pungent odor of a bear's damp pelt and hear the soft, firm tread of its huge feet. He let the spade drop and faced Barry over the little tree. "It's the bear," he whispered, "isn't it?"

Barry nodded dumbly.

"I don't know what to do," mouthed Jacob.

Barry didn't even dare to shrug.

And then Dinah came down the steps with her bucket and exclaimed, "They've come." She might have been announcing the arrival of very ordinary friends, not ghostly wild beasts.

Barry looked over at Dinah but focused instead on the lioness that came walking around the corner of the house. Her head was lowered as though she were following a scent, and her strides were graceful and almost rhyth-mic. When she reached Dinah, she lifted her head, and her eyes flashed an unearthly luminescent gold.

"Look out!" Jacob yelled.

The wolf came bounding out of the trees. He cut across the garden, making straight for Barry. The boy jumped back with a shriek that seemed to stop the wolf in his tracks.

"You've frightened him," Dinah scolded. "Be friendly, Barry. He won't hurt you."

Barry didn't believe that for one minute. He thought, *This is not happening, Barry. Close your eyes, and when you open them, the garden will be empty, except for Dinah, Jacob, and you.*

It didn't work.

Both boys gazed helplessly at Dinah until she became aware of their terror. She had forgotten how the crea-tures must appear to others. To her, they were friendly and protective as long as she stayed where they wanted her. She walked over to the boys, set down her bucket, and commanded, "Put out your hands, both of you, the hand nearest to an animal."

"No way," Barry muttered, but he watched Jacob obeying Dinah's instructions. Extending his left hand, Jacob reached the thick fur between the bear's ears, then he moved his fingers over the wide head in a gentle stroking motion. Without moving, the bear turned his beady black eyes on Jacob, and Jacob, too afraid to remove his hand, continued with his cautious stroking.

The wolf walked closer to Barry and made the boy look at him. It seemed unfair, somehow, that he was being left out of all the fuss. Barry found that the wolf's face was not dangerous at all; he had a lonely, questioning expression that was almost comical. And before he could think twice, Barry was reaching out to touch the wolf's head, if only to take away the sad clown look. Was it possible to make a wolf smile?

The wolf pressed against Barry and sat beside him, making a sound like an anxious dog.

"There," said Dinah. "Now we're all friends!" She

put her bucket beside the little sapling. "One more dig, Jacob, and we'll get the tree."

Jacob picked up the spade, gave a final heave, and the tree tumbled out. He lifted it carefully into Dinah's bucket.

Barry noticed they had formed a circle around the tree. Three animals and three children, like a ceremony.

"What's happening, Dinah?" he asked.

"We're digging up a tree," she told him.

"We've done that. You know what I mean."

"The animals?" She gave a thoughtful sigh and regarded the lioness, who was now resting beside her. "She was the first. The others came later. I can't explain how. If I even try to, they might leave me. I thought they would do anything for me, but they can't kill. Not yet, anyway."

Barry asked hoarsely, "Doesn't anyone notice when they leave the wall?"

"No." Dinah laughed. It was a high, joyful sound that seemed to fill the narrow space between the trees like something tangible that the secluded garden would hold forever. And the boys realized, in the same instant, that they had never heard Dinah laugh before.

They moved carefully past the animals and went into the house. Jacob carried the bucket while Barry supported the tree. Dinah went first with the hurricane lamp. She showed them into the Harp Room, where candles burned in saucers all along the mantelpiece.

"A fuse blew," she explained, "and the light doesn't come on in here anymore. But I like candles, anyway."

Barry looked up at the chandelier. "That's old," he said. "It wasn't made for electricity."

"I'm going to get candles for it," she said. "Tiny white ones like you put on birthday cakes."

"It'll look great," Jacob told her.

They set about making the tree sit upright in its battered and rusty bucket. It looked really good when Dinah had covered the bucket with scarlet paper and hung threads of bottle-top stars from the thin branches.

"Have you got any tree lights?" Barry asked.

"No," said Dinah sharply. "We left them somewhere."

He knew immediately that it was a question he should not have asked, but then he had to go and say the wrong thing again. "You could come over to our place on Christmas Day. We have a great time."

"No," she said fiercely.

Jacob gave Barry a funny sideways glance, and Barry wondered if it were possible for Jacob to understand Dinah better than he did.

"We're having folks over," Dinah explained. "Relatives. We'll be very busy."

Barry looked around the empty room, at the rough floorboards and uncurtained windows. He saw the damp patches on the wall and the cracked plaster ceiling. "Oh," he said.

Dinah stared intently at the strand of silver stars she was looping around the base of her tree. "You can go now," she said without looking up. "Thanks for your help."

They shuffled out, feeling helpless and undignified.

The animals had retreated to the trees. The boys could hear a soft scuffling in the shadows. Barry retrieved his spade while Jacob kicked earth back into the hole he had made.

The shabby cat was crouching beside a sycamore when they went out to the street.

"He's peculiar, that cat," Barry remarked.

"I know," Jacob agreed. "He wants to get into Dinah's garden, but he can't. It's like he's *got* to. Maybe he'll die trying."

"Dinah!" muttered Barry. "She thinks she's the cat's whiskers, she does." He laughed at his own joke, but Jacob didn't seem to get it.

They walked down Anglesey Road in silence, turned a corner, and walked another two blocks, still without speaking. At last Jacob declared, "I'm not following you or anything. I go home this way. My mom's in tonight."

"I know. You said," Barry murmured.

"I forgot to tell you," Jacob went on. "Mrs. Price said my war project was good. Not as good as yours, but better than most other people's. So thanks."

"That's good news," Barry said, and he found himself genuinely pleased for Jacob. "What about Dinah's work?" he asked.

"She did the wrong thing entirely. The wrong war. Imagine!"

"Crazy." Barry felt guilty. But would it have made any difference if he had warned Dinah that she was working on the wrong war? It would not, he decided. Dinah did what she pleased.

When they reached Barry's gate, it seemed quite natural to ask Jacob if he wanted to come in.

"Okay," said Jacob. "Thanks."

Dinah stayed in the Harp Room when the boys had gone. She sat by her tree, admiring the glittering shapes she had made. She opened the window, letting a cool draft rush in and set the silver dancing.

Watching the tree, she felt the empty room blossom around her: the thick brilliant carpet, the heavy curtains, the shining furniture, and, in the corner, Mrs. Gwynne's great golden harp. It *would* happen. It had to.

She was quite alone in the house. Tahira and Karim were out visiting, saying their good-byes. And Rosalie was late.

Dinah went into the kitchen, forgetting the rotten floorboard that had threatened to crack for a week. She tripped and fell against the table. There was nothing in the fridge except milk, margarine, and a piece of cheese. Hoping her mother would bring home something to eat, she cut herself a slice of bread and sat on the table, chewing.

But Rosalie had forgotten the shopping. When she came in, she looked white and strained. Her hair was in a mess and her makeup streaked. "I couldn't get a taxi," she explained. "There's soup in the cupboard. We won't starve."

"How's Gomer?" Dinah asked.

"Better. He'll be out in a couple of days. But he's got to take it easy." She glanced quickly at Dinah. "He wants to go away for Christmas, Di. The doctor thinks it's a good idea."

"Let him!" Dinah leaped up and hugged Rosalie. "We don't need him, Mom."

"I do," Rosalie said quietly.

Dinah drew away, her appetite gone. "I'm going to bed," she said. "There's a tree in the Harp Room if you want to see it."

She went upstairs, dragging her feet. On the first landing, a whole sheet of wallpaper had peeled away from the wall. It lay across the floor, dotted with mildewy chunks of plaster. A thread of water trickled down the exposed bricks and splashed onto the floorboards.

Dinah put her hand on the wet bricks. "Don't fall down before Christmas," she begged.

She stood listening to the dying pulse of Griffin's Castle, wondering how she could get what she wanted and still make Rosalie happy.

A MOUNTAIN
· FAMILY

Dinah never thought that her aunt would provide a solution. But she did in a way. There she was, standing on the top step, shivering in a long red coat, when Dinah got home from school. Auntie June could never have resembled Father Christmas. She was short and blond and rather elegant in a petite way, and yet when Dinah first saw the bright splash of scarlet at the end of the garden, she experienced a tiny flutter of hope, as though the very color could bring about some miracle.

Her aunt turned when she heard the gate close and called out, "Oh, Dinah. I was just about to give up. Where's your mom?"

Dinah ran up the path. "I don't know." She kissed her aunt and let her into the house.

"My God, Dinah, it stinks of damp in here," Auntie June said, staring at the ceiling with pursed lips. A lump of plaster fell onto the mat as Dinah closed the door.

"Would you like to see the tree?" Dinah asked, leading her aunt into the Harp Room.

"Very nice," said Auntie June, giving the room a cursory glance. She backed out, blowing on her hands. "I hope you're getting out of here soon, Dinah."

"We don't have to," Dinah said.

"It's in the cards, I heard. Rosalie phoned your gran last week. Is there a warm room anywhere, Di?"

"The kitchen," Dinah said, showing her aunt the way.

"D'you call this warm?" Auntie June stood two interesting-looking bags against a table leg.

"Don't complain. Please don't complain," said Dinah under her breath. She switched on the electric heater and pulled it close to the chair her aunt had chosen. "It's a good house," she said, "and it warms up really quickly in here. We've got everything we need: a stove, beds, chairs, a bathroom. . . ."

"I should hope so," Auntie June said.

"And hot water," Dinah went on eagerly, "and lots of room. It's a beautiful house, isn't it? They're going to do it up a bit. . . ."

"Should be condemned, I'd say," her aunt commented. "Any chance of a cup of tea, Di?"

Dinah put the kettle on. She stood beside the sink, wondering where the conversation should go next.

"Well," said her aunt with a saccharine smile, "what's been going on, Dinah? Your gran gave me this address, otherwise I'd never have known. Rosalie doesn't give much away, does she?"

"She's got this job," Dinah explained, "and her boss, Mr. Gwynne, he gave us the house. It's his, but he doesn't live here."

"I can see why," muttered Auntie June.

Dinah ignored this. "But Mr. Gwynne isn't very

well just at present. He's in the hospital as a matter of fact. Heart trouble. But he'll be out soon, and he's going to take us somewhere for Christmas. Somewhere grand, like a hotel."

"That's nice. I was going to talk to you about Christmas. I've got your presents here." Auntie June picked up a plastic bag and pulled out two elegantly wrapped presents. Dinah guessed they both contained baskets of soap or bubble bath.

"Thanks," she said. "I've got yours ready upstairs." She ran out, pleased with herself for remembering to wrap them last night.

When she came back into the kitchen, there was a folder of photographs lying on the table. "The latest of Angela and Julie," her aunt told her. "Thought you'd like to see them, Dinah."

"Oh, yes," said Dinah, disgusted by her pretend enthusiasm.

Her aunt began to pass photographs across the

table: Angela and Julie on the beach, Angela on a swing, Julie and a puppy, the new house in Hereford, more beach shots.

"We had such a lovely vacation this year," Auntie June told Dinah. "Sunshine every day."

"Lucky you." Dinah smiled. She had no vacation photos to exchange. "What's this?" She pulled out a small black-and-white photograph.

"Must be your gran's," said her aunt without interest. "I was showing these to her yesterday, and she got out that big tin of old photos. She loves comparing faces." She took the little photograph and squinted at it. "Yes, it's your gran's. It's very old, sixty years or more. Must've got stuck to the back of mine."

"But who are they?"

"My grandmother and grandfather, and that's Mom, your gran. She's the baby he's holding."

"But where?" Dinah snatched back the photograph.

"Up at the farm, I s'pose," said Auntie June with a disapproving frown. "Got any cookies?"

"In the cupboard." Dinah could not move. She heard her aunt get up and rifle through the cupboards, talking to herself or to Dinah. But Dinah, holding the little photograph like a treasure, was entering the place she saw there. She was going through a door into an enchanted country. "Where?" she heard herself ask again.

And from far away she heard her aunt's reply. "Snowdonia. You can see the mountains."

"Yes."

A young couple stood before a drystone wall. They were both dark. He had a shock of black hair blowing across his forehead and a strong, handsome face. If Dinah could have invented a husband for her mother, this was the face she would have given him. The woman was laughing. She was holding her husband's arm and laughing up at the baby, who was patting the air with both hands. Or was she catching blossoms? Because there was an old tree inside the wall, covered in flowers. Beyond the tree there was a white farmhouse, and behind the house a mountain, its summit still white with snow. Sheep dotted the mountainside below the snowmelt, sheep like white petals. It was the truest family Dinah had ever seen. Their happiness leaped out at her.

"Olwen Gwalchmai," Dinah murmured.

"That's it," Auntie June declared, dunking her cookie. "Gwalchmai, what a name. Gran was glad to change it when she married."

"I like it," said Dinah. "I think it's wonderful."

"Well, there we are." Her aunt sniffed.

"Did you ever go there?"

"To the farm? No, never. It was a mucky place, by all accounts. Your gran wasn't happy there."

"Why?"

"You were always a devil for questions, Dinah! But it's not natural at your age. Not becoming. Gran was lonely, and I'm not surprised. He made her speak Welsh all the time."

"So what? I'm learning Welsh. It's beautiful."

"You're impossible, you are!" Auntie June studied Dinah's face for a moment and then glanced back at the photograph. "Your gran was right. You do look a bit like him. He came to Cardiff when you were a baby. He brought a kitten from the farm. Daft, really! He lost it, of course. Lost himself, too, Gran said."

"He tried to find us?" Dinah asked incredulously.

"He thought Rosalie would take you to live on the farm after Billy ran off. Imagine! Rosalie's the same as me. We like bright lights, nice clothes, fun!" She winked at Dinah. "Rosalie couldn't live on a farm. She loves the city."

"I don't," Dinah said.

"That may be," Auntie June retorted. "But your mom's had a tough time looking after you. She's given up a lot for your sake. She deserves a break!"

"I know, and I want her to have one. It's just . . ." Dinah struggled for words. She wanted to ask for help, yet knowing her aunt wouldn't provide it, she was not going to beg. "It's just that I don't know how to help Mom right now."

"You'll find a way," asserted Auntie June. "Got a bit of paper, love? I'll write your mom a note. I can't stay any longer."

"Can I keep the photo?"

"'Course. Your gran was going to chuck it out."

How could she? How could you throw away the past when it was a priceless treasure? Dinah pulled a pad from her bookbag, tore out a sheet, and handed it to her aunt.

With a sleek silver pen, June wrote:

Dear Rosalie,
Sorry to have missed you.
Hope you liked the present and thanks for yours.
Glad you're getting away from this place for
Christmas. It's a bit of a dump, Rosalie. Unhealthy.
Hope you find somewhere else soon.

Let me know your new address when you do.

You must come over to Hereford one day.

John sends love, as do I.

June

Auntie June slipped her note under the sugar bowl and said, "See she gets it, Dinah. I'll be off now. Have a nice Christmas, love."

Dinah regarded the sheet of lined paper. It was practically shouting ideas at her.

A quick hug and a peck on the cheek and her aunt was gone. Dinah didn't wait to see if she made it through the garden. She had work to do. She closed the door quickly and ran back to the kitchen. In her bag she still kept the railway timetable she had picked up in Swansea three months ago. Dinah pulled it out and quickly scanned the vertical rows of times and stations until she found something suitable. Then, placing her aunt's note on the table, she sat down and tore out another sheet of paper. For a moment she scrutinized the curls and loops of her aunt's writing. She chewed her pen while the message she wanted took shape in her head.

Ten minutes later, in a perfect copy of her aunt's handwriting, she had written another letter to Rosalie. The first two sentences and the last one were the same; otherwise, it was pure Dinah.

Dear Rosalie,

Sorry to have missed you.

Hope you like the present and thanks for yours.

Dinah tells me you're going away for Christmas.

I've asked her to come to us, and she says she'd love to. The girls are dying to see her again.

Put her on the 10:40 on Thursday, and we'll meet her in Hereford. She can stay a week.

Have a good time and give us a ring when you get back.

John sends love, as do I.

June

Dinah sat back, pleased with her work, but as she tore the first message into strips, she felt a shiver of apprehension. It all depended on Mrs. Gwynne now. She would have to come. If she did not, Dinah *would* be alone with the animals.

"So what?" she said aloud. "There's nothing to be afraid of. I wanted them here, so why should they hurt me?"

But Mrs. Gwynne *would* come.

Rosalie seemed better when she came in, but Dinah couldn't wait to see the effect her forged note would have.

"Look," she said, holding out the message that her aunt had not written. "Auntie June was here. She left a note."

Watching Rosalie's face soften with relief as she read it, Dinah knew that she had given her mother the Christmas present she had most wanted.

"It's wonderful, Di," Rosalie exclaimed. "D'you really want to go? You didn't get on so well with Angela last time."

"We're older. Of course I want to," Dinah lied. "It'll be great. Write and say it's okay, Mom, and I'll mail the letter on my way to school."

Rosalie wrote at once. She told her sister what luck it was that her invitation to Dinah had come just then. Because now Rosalie could go away with Gomer Gwynne to a hotel by the sea, where Gomer would get well again. And Rosalie would walk along the shore and come back to sit beside log fires and be cosseted by waiters. "Gomer's been so good to us," she wrote, "so generous and kind, so I owe it to him, really. I'll be a kind of nurse."

Dinah stood beside her mother and made sure that Rosalie mentioned the train. "Dinah will be on the 10:40 on Thursday morning." She turned to Dinah. "Was that right?" Dinah nodded. "And she looks forward to it very much."

It was a long letter for Rosalie, and Dinah was almost sorry that it would have to be destroyed. When it had been safely tucked inside an envelope, Dinah showed Rosalie the photograph.

"I remember that. It's nice, isn't it?" Rosalie said. "Your great-grandparents."

"Why was Olwen buried here and not in the mountains?" Dinah asked.

Rosalie frowned at the photograph. "Olwen's folks lived here. They're all gone now. She was visiting them when she died. Just took ill with the flu or something, and that was it. Sad, isn't it?"

"What about him?" Dinah held the picture closer to her mother, wanting her to see . . . What? A brave, kind face or the man beyond those hardy features, a hero? "My great-grandfather?"

"What about him, Di?"

"He came to find us once. Did you know that?"

"Gran might have told me."

"Perhaps he's still waiting there, lonely on his mountain." She covered Olwen Gwalchmai with her hand. "Without a wife, but there in that same house, with the wind and the sheep and snow on the mountain. Why doesn't anyone go and see?"

"I don't know, Dinah. I suppose we were a bit afraid of him."

"Why?"

"Perhaps Gran wanted us to be. She was always telling us how stern he was, quoting from the Bible, making her learn things. Funny, really." Rosalie gave a wry smile. "If Gran had been more like you, she might have been happy."

"Could I go, Mom, one day? It's where we came from, after all!"

"It's miles away, Di!" Rosalie wanted to make a list of the clothes she would need for her vacation. She didn't have time to talk about an old man she could hardly remember. "We've lost touch. It's too late now."

"It's not too late," said Dinah fiercely.

꙾   ꙾   ꙾

After supper Dinah took the photograph up to her room and propped it against the bedside lamp. Rosalie had tried to make the mountain seem far away, but it wasn't, not really. There was a thread as strong and fine as silk linking her forever with that wild clear place and the happiness of Olwen and Tomos Gwalchmai. When her great-grandparents had smiled at the camera, sixty years ago, the moment belonged to Dinah. It was part of her. No one could take it away or say that it had not happened.

She forgot to say good night to the animals and slept fitfully, kept awake by images of her own white fingers tearing paper, of Griffin's Castle tumbling down and wild beasts prowling through the debris. And the only sound was a distant, melancholy wail that could have been the wind, or a baby crying, or even a cat's plaintive call. And then mountain snow had come, like flying stars, covering them all in a soft, heavy blanket of silence.

Dinah woke up feeling ill. She told herself it was guilt. For more than a week, she would have to keep up the pretense that she was going to Hereford for Christmas. Gomer had won. That was the most bitter pill of all.

She took her mother a cup of tea, and, waving the letter addressed to June, she said, "I'll mail it on my way to school."

"You're early, love." Rosalie peered blearily from the covers.

"Extra work to do at school!" Dinah told her. She wanted to get it over with as soon as she could. "Bye!"

There was a mailbox on the corner before she turned onto Elias Road. Dinah was alone on the street, but she went through the motions, putting the white envelope into the mouth of the box, then quickly pulling it back and slipping it into her pocket. When she reached the trash can outside the school gates, she tore the letter into shreds and dropped them in.

"What're you doing?" asked a voice.

Dinah swung around. "Are you spying on me?"

"No!" Jacob Rose hopped back a pace. "I'm just early

because Mom's at home, so I didn't have far to come, but I forgot and came out at the same time as I do when I'm down at my auntie's and . . ."

"Okay, okay," Dinah said curtly, and strode away.

"Hey, did you know that cat had followed you?" he called.

Dinah stopped and looked around. Jacob was right. There it was, crouching by the fence on the other side of the road. She scowled at it, yelled, "Shoo!" and turned her back.

Jacob sighed. He had bought her a present, a pencil tin with a lioness painted on the lid. It was a brilliant choice, but she just didn't deserve it, moody so-and-so. He decided to ask Barry's advice.

At recess Dinah walked around with a couple of girls, not contributing much to their conversation but trying to erase the sick, gritty feeling in the pit of her stomach. She noticed Barry and Jacob kicking a ball up to the playing fields and felt a twinge of satisfaction. She had brought them together, after all.

On her way home, Dinah remembered that it was Wednesday. The Maliks were leaving on Thursday. Tonight she would have to say good-bye.

Lights shone out from the basement, and music issued faintly into the garden. It was a dark, dreary day. The animals would arrive very soon.

Rosalie was in the kitchen, cooking up something good. She was singing, too, happier now than she had been for weeks. And Dinah felt suddenly distanced from her mother by the giant step she had taken, the lie that seemed as wide as the world. She couldn't talk to Rosalie yet, afraid that her expression might somehow betray her plans.

She ran upstairs to fetch the Maliks' gifts. She had wrapped them in red tissue paper, glued tinfoil flowers in a corner, and printed the names with a silver pen. They looked small but exciting, she thought, as the silver patterns glinted under the hall light.

The Maliks were packing. Clothes and baby gear

were strewn over every chair. But they stopped for Dinah and made tea. Dinah held her present out to Yusuf. He took it solemnly and unwrapped it while his parents murmured advice. "Be careful, Yusuf. It looks so special. You are lucky."

He took out the little dragon and smiled.

"It's a Welsh dragon," Dinah explained, "so that you'll remember us."

Yusuf nodded.

"And here's something for Maryam! You can hear it, listen!" She shook the small red bundle, and a bell tinkled inside it, making the baby stretch out her hands toward it.

Karim's smile broke into laughter, and then they were all laughing and Tahira was pressing something into Dinah's arms, a length of soft chiffon, the color of a summer sky, embroidered with silver thread.

Dinah held it out, speechless with delight.

"And you will remember us?" Tahira said.

"I'll never forget you!"

"I want you to write to us, Dinah!" Tahira tucked a small sheet of paper into Dinah's hand. "It's our address in Canada. We're living with Karim's brother for a while. And you must tell us where you are because you won't stay here much longer, I think."

"I don't know. I don't know where else I'll be going," Dinah said.

All at once the room was empty of laughter, and Karim said gravely, "You must leave here, Dinah. You know it, surely. The house is falling down. It was wrong of Gomer to let people live here. If I had known . . . Look!" He pressed his fist into the wall, and damp plaster crumbled to the floor. "There's danger here. Terrible danger for you."

"Yes, yes, I know," Dinah said quickly. "It's all right. Gomer's taking Mom away soon, Mom *and* me, but I don't know where."

"*And* you, Dinah?" Tahira looked searchingly into her face.

"Yes, me. And anyway, the animals are here, so I'm safe."

"The animals can't keep you safe, Dinah," Karim said.

"Have you seen them?" she asked hopefully.

"I know that they are there," he replied. "But you mustn't rely on them. Don't let them surround you, Dinah. They are wild and very strong."

"I know," Dinah agreed. "Will you write back to me?"

"Of course!" Tahira spoke so fervently that Dinah ran and hugged her.

"I've got to go now. Mom's home," she said. "I expect she'll come and say good-bye tomorrow, but I'll be in school when you go, so I'm saying it now." She walked quickly into the passage and began to mount the steps.

"Good-bye, Dinah!" they called after her, and little Yusuf followed her, flapping the hand that still held the dragon.

When Dinah looked down from the hall door, they

were gathered at the bottom of the stairs. Karim was holding the baby. Dinah waved and closed the door between them.

They were good friends, and I'll never see them again, she thought, wondering if she should have warned them not to try to leave at night.

But then it was only Dinah whom the animals wanted to keep.

DINAH ALONE

Jacob told himself that he was happy. His mother would be at home for most of the holiday, his father would be in on Christmas Eve, and Uncle Tad had bought him something special. Barry had promised to come by with his electric keyboard, and that they would definitely go to a movie together.

But something nagged at Jacob, an ache that would not go away. There was something wrong with Dinah Jones. It puzzled and worried him. He couldn't give the present he had bought her to anyone else. It belonged to her already in a way because of the lioness.

He saw Dinah swinging away from the school gates on the last day of the term and called out, "Hey! Dinah! Dinah Jones!"

She ignored him and increased her pace, her back very straight and determined looking. So he ran after her and leaped in her path, shouting, "Hey, are you deaf?"

She stared at him, her eyes coldly ferocious, but he couldn't let her pass without putting his request.

"Shall we come and see you over the holiday, Barry and me?" He included Barry because he knew that Barry had something for Dinah, too, a box of colored pencils. She had asked, so often, to borrow his.

"No!" Her savage expression reminded Jacob of the lioness.

"But why? We wouldn't . . ."

"We're going away," she said flatly.

"You said that relatives were coming."

"Our plans have changed." She brushed past him and began to run.

Jacob called, "What about the animals, Dinah?" Anything to stop her. It didn't work. She ran faster.

On the other side of the street, the cat ran with her, like her diminished shadow.

Barry caught up with Jacob and asked, "Was that Dinah?"

"Yes," murmured Jacob. "I asked if we could go over to her place before Christmas, but she said no."

"We'll go, anyway," said Barry.

"Something's wrong," Jacob declared. "It's not just the animals. I mean, that's bad enough, but two days ago I caught her tearing up a letter. She threw the pieces in a trash can. She didn't know I was watching, and when I asked what she was doing, she jumped and looked angry and frightened, all at the same time."

Barry considered this piece of news while he scratched the bridge of his nose. "I'll come over to your house after tea," he said.

"Great!" Jacob didn't attempt to hide his pleasure. "Mom says it's going to snow." He pressed his cold knuckles to his lips and blew on them.

"Yeah!" cried Barry, zooming off. "We'll have a white Christmas."

The chill inside Griffin's Castle seemed to strike deeper now that the Maliks had left. They had been the safe foundation that had kept the walls steady. Without them, the house began to teeter, threatening to collapse.

All of Rosalie's cheerful singing could not banish the gloom that crept over Dinah during the long weekend after her friends had left.

"I can't believe you miss going to school," her mother chided. "Why don't you have a friend around or something?"

"They're all busy," Dinah lied. She looked at the cracked kitchen ceiling and added, "Besides, the house isn't very welcoming."

"I know, love. But Gomer will have us out of here as soon as Christmas is over."

"Will he?" Dinah already felt guilty for betraying the

house. Supposing it had heard her. It might lose hope and fall down before Mrs. Gwynne could come home again.

"Where will he put us next time?" she inquired.

Rosalie stacked a neat pile of laundry on the ironing board. "Listen, Di! I wasn't going to tell you this until, well, everything was settled, but I can trust you to keep a secret for a while, can't I?"

"There's no one to tell," said Dinah.

"There's Auntie June, for a start. You know what she's like."

"Oh, yes." Dinah nodded, remembering where she was supposed to be going.

"Gomer and I are going to get married when he's . . . recovered. And he's already much better." Rosalie's face brimmed with happiness.

Dinah didn't want to spoil it for her, but she couldn't help exclaiming, "He doesn't like me, Mom. And I don't like him. I never will because I know he's a crook."

"He's not a crook," Rosalie suddenly exploded. "I've

had enough of you, Dinah Jones. Gomer's good to me. He's everything I need, but you can't see that, can you? You're a selfish little beast. You never gave him a chance."

"He never gave me one." Dinah fought back. "He's cruel, and he's greedy, and there'll be no room for me in that one-bedroom apartment!"

"Who says we're going to live there?"

"Wherever it is, he won't want me!" Dinah cried. "He hates me, Mom!"

"I can't say I blame him," Rosalie screamed.

She bundled the laundry onto the table and folded the ironing board with a crash.

Dinah ran to her room.

A few snowflakes floated airily through the beam of light outside her window, but when Dinah looked down into the garden, there was no hint of snow. Like the animals, the snowflakes were phantoms.

Perhaps the animals could read her thoughts. They

were not phantoms. They paced before the gate, blurred forms in the gloom, determined to be real.

On Monday Rosalie went shopping. She came back dripping with bags. Spreading the contents over her bed, she invited Dinah to admire her bargains. Among the colorful piles that made up Rosalie's holiday wardrobe, Dinah found a new bag for herself, a long velvet skirt, and a white blouse.

"Thanks, Mom, they're perfect." She kissed her mother. They were trying to be friends again before they were parted.

"I'm not having you look like a poor relation at June's," said Rosalie. "Angela and Julie will be dressed up to the nines."

"You bet," Dinah agreed. The blouse and skirt would not be wasted. She would wear them for Mrs. Gwynne.

"I want you to be happy, Di, you know that, don't you?" said Rosalie, hugging her very tight.

"We'll both be happy, Mom," Dinah told her.

Later she made a Christmas card for Mrs. Gwynne. She painted Griffin's Castle as it should have been, with gutters mended, and cracks sealed, the front door polished, and every window properly glazed. And on either side of the house, she put rows of Christmas trees, every one adorned with glowing candles.

On Tuesday Dinah cut sprays of foliage from the cypress trees and laid them along the mantelpiece and the picture rail in the Harp Room. Then she strung feathery sprigs over the kitchen cupboards and even on the door handles. For days she had been eyeing a holly tree in one of the derelict gardens down the street. She felt entitled to the clusters of bright berries, for they belonged to no one else.

She wore Tahira's chiffon scarf for the expedition, tucking it into the top of her coat so that the silvery patterns glittered around her face. She came back with armfuls of holly, the spiky leaves still glistening with frost. There was a bitter wind that tried to tear her plunder away, but she clasped the holly tighter, stabbing her hands and face.

The cat hobbled painfully after her. He kept close to the walls, for he knew that he had no weight to keep him from being blown into the road. His ribs protruded through his thin fur, and one of his paws was swollen around a thorn embedded in his pad. The only food he could find was frozen, and the ice had seared his tongue and made his throat ache.

Dinah poked her precious holly in the drafty gaps around the window frames. Then she tied bunches to the banisters and the curved newel post at the bottom of the stairs.

When Rosalie came home, she gazed at the greenery in astonishment. "What's it all for, Dinah?" she asked. "There'll be nobody here."

"Someone might come," Dinah said, "to visit us before we go away."

Rosalie shrugged. "Gomer's so much better!" she

announced. "A taxi will pick me up at ten o'clock on Thursday and take me to the airport. Oh, Di, we're flying. I can't believe this is happening."

"You can drop me at the station, then," said Dinah. "Excellent timing."

"Everything's going to be all right!" Rosalie squeezed her daughter desperately.

"Yes," said Dinah, clinging tight.

The wind roared through the night, and loose shingles tumbled off the roof. The sound, amplified over Dinah's head, was like crashing boulders. Outside, the animals howled disconsolately beneath the thrashing trees.

In the morning, the bathroom pipes had frozen. Rosalie attacked them with a kettle of boiling water, and there were little explosions as the copper fractured and water splashed onto the cold linoleum.

"Darn!" said Rosalie. "Thank goodness we're getting out of here."

"Turn the water off at the mains," Dinah advised.

"I want a bath," wailed Rosalie.

"Then put a bowl under the leak and have your bath if you want to freeze to death," said Dinah. "I'm going out." She had decided to visit Mrs. Gwynne and issue her invitation.

Roxburgh Street looked very festive. There were colored lights and Christmas trees in nearly every window. St. Garmon's Home had a large wreath on the door, decorated with red ribbons and silver bells. And, framed by crimson curtains, a Christmas tree stood in the ground-floor window.

Dinah rang the bell. Betty answered it. Today she wore large hoop earrings and a long purple skirt.

"I've come to see Mrs. Gwynne," Dinah explained. "I'm Dinah. You're Betty, aren't you?"

The woman smiled indulgently. "I remember you. Mr. Gwynne instructed us not to allow any more visits. He told us all about you."

Dinah flushed but carried on boldly. "He's been in

the hospital, but now he's better, and we want Mrs. Gwynne to come to her old home for Christmas. It would be good for her to be among all her own furniture and stuff, and she could play the harp again." Dinah stopped abruptly. Betty was staring at her uneasily.

"I thought everything had gone, love. That's what she told us. The house is empty!"

Dinah looked away. If only she hadn't mentioned the harp. She had been very stupid.

"You'd better come in," Betty said kindly.

Dinah stepped inside. The hall was decorated with paper streamers, and mistletoe hung above the staircase.

"Please can I see her?" Dinah begged. "I've brought a card." She held out her homemade envelope.

"Wait a minute, love," Betty relented. "I can't see that a quick visit would hurt. But don't talk about the house, will you?"

Betty walked briskly down the corridor and into

the room at the end. Dinah followed and looked through the open door. There were hundreds of cards strung across the room and crowding the mantelpiece. Mrs. Gwynne was sitting in the same place, wearing the same violet colors. Betty said something to her, then looked up and beckoned Dinah over.

"She's not quite herself today," Betty warned. "She might not know you. I'll be back in five minutes." She left Dinah and Mrs. Gwynne together.

Dinah took her seat on the other side of the table. She decided to talk about school first, and then the new clothes she had been given. Mrs. Gwynne stared into space, giving no indication that she could even hear Dinah. So Dinah clasped the papery-looking hand that rested on the table and said, "Will you come for Christmas, Mrs. Gwynne? I could fetch you when you've had your lunch. I'll make it warm enough. . . ." She couldn't go on without talking about the house, and she had promised not to.

The old woman turned her head and, smiling at

Dinah, said, "Oh, no, I must stay here. We're having a party."

"But after the party, for a cup of tea and mince pies. We could read *The Jungle Book*." The desperate tone in Dinah's voice began to upset Mrs. Gwynne, who snatched her hand away.

"I don't want to," she said stubbornly.

"Please . . ."

"We have a very nice time here," snapped Mrs. Gwynne. "I like it."

Dinah gazed mutely at the rigid profile and pushed her decorated envelope across the table. Mrs. Gwynne gave it a cursory glance, then looked away.

"It's a Christmas card," Dinah said quietly. "I made it for you."

The old woman took it, tore open the envelope, and pulled out the card.

"It's . . ." Dinah stopped herself, remembering she had been forbidden to mention the house.

But Mrs. Gwynne knew immediately what Dinah

had painted. She gazed at Griffin's Castle, her face softening. She touched the silver glitter that decorated the roof and traced the outline of the house with her finger. She turned to Dinah, her pale eyes glistening, and said, "Not fir trees, dear. They weren't there. It was all lilacs and wild cherry."

Betty approached. "Oh, dear," she whispered, seeing Mrs. Gwynne's expression.

"I'm sorry." Dinah stood up. "I didn't talk about the house. It was the card."

"Never mind. You'd better leave now, Dinah."

She took Dinah's hand and led her quickly through the room. A few elderly people watched her progress, and three or four called out, "Merry Christmas," one after the other, like parrots.

But Mrs. Gwynne didn't say a word. She was still gazing at Dinah's card.

In the hall, Dinah begged again, "Could she come, please? I know the harp and everything is gone, but I would make it really nice for her."

Betty shook her head. "It's not a good idea. I'm sorry. It's a strange time of year for them." She nodded at the closed door behind her. "Some get upset. They remember their families as they were, a long time ago. If Mrs. Gwynne saw her house again, with none of the things she loved in it, well, Dinah, it would set her back a bit. We don't want that, do we?"

"No," said Dinah quietly.

"But it was kind of you to think of her, and after Christmas I'm sure we can arrange another visit. You run along now and have a lovely time with your family."

"All right." Dinah shuffled toward the front door, and when Betty opened it, she walked out, dragging her feet.

Betty watched the girl trudging down the drive, her shoulders hunched and hands stuffed in her pockets. Hadn't someone said that Mrs. Gwynne's old house was falling down, about to become a ruin?

Betty closed the door. There was something

disturbing about Dinah's face, but Betty was too involved with her old people to concern herself with Dinah's problems. Already someone was shouting for her. Mr. Graves had probably spilled his tea again.

On Thursday morning, Dinah woke early. She packed her new bag with everything a girl might need for a week in another house. It looked so convincing, she almost believed that she was going to stay with June.

Rosalie took hours to dress. She finally emerged with five minutes to spare. She carried a large new suitcase and matching overnight bag, both presents from Gomer.

Dinah filled the kettle and a large bowl with cold water. "In case it freezes again before we come back," she said. Then she turned off the water at the mains and put a message in a bottle for the milkman, just as though she wouldn't be back for a week.

The taxi arrived at ten precisely. Dinah and Rosalie

didn't talk on the way to the station. Already Dinah felt distanced from her mother by a thousand miles. But when the station came into view, Dinah suddenly asked, "Will you go and see Mrs. Gwynne, Mom? I mean, you'll be related if you marry Gomer. Make him let you, please!"

Rosalie wasn't perfect, but she never made promises she couldn't keep. "All right, Di," she said. "If it means so much to you, I promise I'll visit his mom."

They swept into the street in front of the station, and Dinah threw her arms around Rosalie. "Have a great time, Mom!" she murmured.

She jumped out of the taxi, slamming the door after her, and stood at the curb as Rosalie was whisked away, her pale hand fluttering in the rear window. Dinah waved back briefly and walked into the station.

She remained on the concourse for ten minutes, pretending to consult the departures information and her watch. But no one seemed interested in a girl on her own. No one knew she was tall for her age and had trapped herself into a solitary Christmas.

Striding purposefully out of the station, she made her way up St. Mary Street, toward the castle. The city sidewalks were crowded with last-minute shoppers, flushed and anxious, hunting for bargains. Dinah wished she had not filled her new bag so convincingly. It was large and heavy and dragged on her arm. She had to keep changing hands. When she reached Castle Street, she put the bag down and glanced quickly to her left, where the animal wall led to Cardiff Bridge and the River Taff. The animals were all there, as far as she could see, and their effigies would still be there at night, deceiving the world into believing that they were only stone and did not have spirits that fled, at dusk, to guard another castle.

Dinah picked up her bag and began to walk toward the wide tree-lined road called Boulevard de Nantes. It led to the National Museum, but she hoped to catch a bus before she got that far. As she approached the museum, she saw two boys sitting on the shallow steps. She turned away quickly, but they had seen her and came running across.

"Hey!" called Barry. "Dinah Jones, where are you going?"

It was useless to try and escape with the heavy bag. She dumped it on the ground with a sigh.

"I thought you said you were going away," Jacob said accusingly.

"I am!" She stamped her foot. "I've just been shopping. The taxi's coming for us this afternoon. We're flying."

"Flying?" Both boys looked at her in disbelief.

Dinah glared back defiantly. "It's not so unusual," she said.

"D'you want to come into the museum with us?" asked Barry. "There are some great dinosaurs."

"No," Dinah almost shouted. "Of course I don't."

She scooped the bag off the ground and turned up Museum Avenue.

Jacob paced beside her. "Can I give you a hand with that? It looks heavy." He tried to take the handle of Dinah's bag, but she pulled away from him.

"Go away," she cried. "Leave me alone."

Jacob came to a halt while she strode ahead. She thought the boys had abandoned her and gone to see their dinosaurs, but when she was halfway up the avenue, a voice called, "We'll come around later, in case you've changed your plans again! We've got presents for you. Shall we put them in your mailbox?"

"If you want," she shouted without looking back. "But I won't be there!"

She caught a bus going north and jumped off when she recognized a building near Anglesey Road. The bus rolled away, and Dinah watched it for a moment, as though its busy, harassed passengers might be the last people she would ever see.

Anglesey Road was silent except for the wind that still tormented the empty buildings, flinging echoes down derelict stairwells, shaking the rotten window frames, and sighing its way through the wild gardens.

She ran the last few feet to Griffin's Castle, afraid of the desolate road behind her and the sinister empty houses. When she grasped the gate, she felt the real world slide away, as though she were balanced on ice.

The cat that was walking toward her spun out of focus and became a dark smudge in the frost.

Dinah could never remember how she had hauled herself through the gate. She could only recall fumbling at the lock while the garden pressed at her back, its breath dense and chill. When she closed the door against the cold, she felt as though she had battled through a force field.

She sat in the kitchen, unable to think. She had planned, with such care, the meals she would eat while Rosalie was away. The cupboard was crammed with tins: corned beef, beans, and vegetables. She wouldn't starve.

What did people do on Christmas Eve?

There was some smokeless fuel left in the bag Karim had bought. She could light a fire. She could watch television or even go out again. The library would be open.

But Dinah did none of these things. She found herself exhausted by the decision she had made. She took a chair into the Harp Room and sat watching the garden, waiting for darkness and the animals. *No one in the world,* she thought, *knows that I am here.*

What happens on Christmas Eve?

Someone in a red coat finds his way into your home and leaves the gifts you've always wanted tied to the foot of your bed. But only if you are asleep.

Dinah would not be asleep. *Perhaps I am not here at all,* she thought. *Perhaps this house is balanced between the past and the future and has vanished for a moment, while it tries to return to its former glory, instead of the pile of rubble that everyone has decided it should become. And if I can't get back to the* mountain where my family came from, maybe I can drift into the past with Griffin's Castle and creep into the family that lived here eighty years ago, just as though I belonged to them.

As if to confirm this notion of traveling into the past, the outside world began to change. Shapes and angles shifted, subtly at first, as though it were only Dinah's perception of them that had altered. But after a few minutes, she knew that she was not mistaken. The trees had grown. She could not see where they began and ended.

But where were the hedges of lilac and cherry? The fir trees had not been planted eighty years ago. There was a forest growing round Dinah that could only belong to the future.

She watched the mysterious and brooding swell of vegetation for a long time before she felt compelled to explore the strange place that seemed to be surrounding her. But at last she opened the front door and stepped down into the garden. Under her feet, the icy ground rustled like splintered glass. The trees reached through a canopy of snow and vanished.

"Where are you?" she called.

And then she heard them, prowling in the forest, brutal and furtive. Dinah tried to run down the ribbon of light that must have been a path, but she could not move.

Mist claimed the gate and the garden wall; it swallowed the streetlamps and the houses across the road. Moonlight washed over the roof, so strong that Griffin's Castle seemed to disappear behind a sheath of silver. The trees moaned and leaned in the wind that suddenly swept down from the stars. And Dinah, breathless with cold, gazed about her arctic forest, wondering if the animals were turning the world to stone.

The Call
of the Cat

Jacob was playing Scrabble with Uncle Tadeusz. They sat on opposite sides of the kitchen table while Mrs. Rose fussed around the oven, trying to get her mince pies right.

In the room next door, Auntie Mair and Jacob's father were talking quietly together. Occasionally they would laugh, and Auntie Mair would sing a familiar carol.

It had been the same last Christmas and the one before that. Jacob enjoyed the sense of security that this gave him. Nothing had changed. And then Dinah Jones slipped into his thoughts. He saw her battling against the wind, her body bent toward the weight of the heavy bag, her thin legs moving awkwardly.

"She's still there," he murmured. "I know she is."

"Who's there?" his uncle inquired, finishing the game with a triumphant, "There! You're not concentrating, boy."

"Dinah Jones," Jacob said. "I'm no good at words tonight." He went to the window and looked down the street. The sky was dark and the air filled with a fluttering whiteness. It was beginning to snow.

"I think I should go and see her."

"You're not going anywhere, Jacob Rose," his mother said. "It's Christmas Eve. Bedtime for you, otherwise . . ."

"I know. I know," Jacob said, giving in.

Barry and Josh were wrapping presents for their parents. Josh had made a terrible mess with his mother's bubble bath. The paper had split at the side, and the lid still showed. Barry gave it a second covering of green tissue paper and stuck a ribbon over the gap at the top.

"Great! Great! Great!" yelled Josh, scooping up his motley assortment of packages.

Barry followed Josh downstairs. Kevin was inspecting the presents under the tree. It was the tallest Christmas tree their father had ever bought; the crowning star almost touched the ceiling.

While his brothers rearranged the pile of presents, Barry stood back to survey the magical sweep of lights and tinsel. He wondered why the tree's presence was so necessary and so special and why to be without it was unthinkable. And, all at once, he saw Dinah's tiny sapling and the bottle-top stars shining bravely against the spare green foliage.

He looked away from his fine tree and saw a cloud of snowflakes whirling past the window, but the excitement this should have caused did not come to Barry.

Dinah Jones was in trouble. It was no use telling himself he was mistaken or that it was none of his business. He knew it and no one else did, except for Jacob Rose, so they were responsible. But Barry also knew that neither of them would leave home tonight.

I'll go tomorrow, Barry told himself, ignoring the voice in his head that warned him it might be too late.

Dinah went back into the house. The lights had gone out, and when she pressed the switch in the hall, it clicked uselessly under her finger. The electricity had failed again.

The pipes in the kitchen groaned and rattled, and a noxious smell came from the sink.

Dinah lit a candle and took it into the Harp Room. She brought the comforter and pillow from Rosalie's bed and laid them on the floor beside the window. She couldn't bring herself to climb to the top of the house. The weather was tearing at the roof; she could hear rafters cracking and shingles sliding and falling.

Griffin's Castle is dying, she thought, *but at least I am here to keep it company.*

The garden was bright with ice and moonlight. It shone into the room where Dinah lay, showing her, for the last time, the patterns on the Persian carpet, the velvet covers, the small gleaming tables, and Mrs. Gwynne's great harp, all silver-gray now, all turned to stone.

Dinah thought of her lost family on the mountain. When she fell asleep, she was certain she could hear their voices.

She woke up before the sky was light. The hands on her watch had not moved since midnight, and Dinah wondered if time had stopped. She tried to find her pulse, imagining that the flow of blood from her heart had frozen. But there was something there, still warm, still beating.

She stood up, drawing the comforter around her shoulders. Her hands were blue, and her breath steamed in tiny clouds against the windowpane. Frost had decorated the glass with a sheet of sparkling stars.

Dinah scratched at the ice until she had cleared a patch of glass the size of a small porthole. Peering into the garden, the first thing she saw was the lynx. It was sitting perfectly still, a few feet from the window, and it was looking up at her, a pale lynx with a fixed inscrutable gaze. Beyond the lynx, there was a leopard, in almost the same position. And there was another creature beside it, a beaver perhaps.

Letting the comforter fall from her shoulders, Dinah tore at the frost, widening her view of the garden, enthralled and terrified by what she might see.

She saw an ape and its child on a low branch and, perched on the gate, a tall gray vulture. The raccoons were hiding in the frosty trees; she could just make out their small puzzled faces. The hyena was watching them from below.

They are all here, Dinah thought. *This is our celebration, theirs and mine.*

She put on her coat and ran to the front door. When she opened it, she found the bear, the wolf, and the lioness, looking up at her from the foot of the steps.

The wolf's quizzical expression had hardened into something sly and secretive. The bear's black eyes had narrowed; his shoulders resembled a slab of granite. Only the lioness seemed unchanged, but then she had always looked ruthless and unpredictable.

Dinah drew a deep breath. "Good morning," she said, and, to her surprise, added, "I want to visit my great-grandmother this morning. Will you let me through?"

They didn't move an inch but regarded her with even more intensity. Their coats had lost the bright silky look and seemed mysteriously bleached in the dead light.

She didn't want to offend them by suggesting they were made of stone, but the sudden desire to be near Olwen Gwalchmai had become overwhelming. She felt she would say anything to make the animals move.

"You can't keep me here," she said. "If you don't move, I won't believe in you anymore."

She took three determined steps down to them, putting out her hand to thrust the animals aside. But she encountered an invisible barrier. She threw her weight against it, not caring if she fell into the teeth of the silent creatures, but she was flung back with such savage force, she could only lie spread-eagled on the steps, shocked and terrified.

"It's me," she whispered. "Dinah. You must let me go!"

They didn't seem to hear her.

Dinah knew then that she was their prisoner and would never reach the gate where the vulture waited.

There was only one way out. "I shall fly," she announced. "You'll see!"

She ran inside and mounted the rotting staircase. Every tread seemed to crack and splinter under her feet. It was like climbing a mountain. She could see a patch of sky through the roof of her bedroom. The floor was littered with broken shingles, and a beam had fallen across the bed. Her cuttings had peeled away from the wall and lay in wet heaps, their words and pictures blurred into insignificance.

Dinah picked her way through the rubble and

reached the window. She didn't have to open it. The frame had cracked and fallen out. It hung in the air by a single hinge. Dinah put one foot on the sill. She felt quite certain that she could fly.

She glanced down into the garden. The animals seemed unaware of her intention. How she would surprise them!

She drew her other foot up to the sill, balancing herself with one hand on the crumbling brickwork. *What would it be like,* she wondered, *to soar through the white dawn sky?* She *would* reach Olwen Gwalchmai. She felt invincible.

"Now!" whispered Dinah, and let go.

At that instant a sound struck through her, more wild and haunting than any cry from the creatures below. It came from a cat, far away, but its fear caught at Dinah and opened her eyes. Shaking with horror at what might have been, Dinah stepped back into the safety of her room, stumbled blindly down the dangerous stairs and out into the gray garden. This time she had something to help her battle through the force that surrounded her. She had the power and the anger of the cat beyond the gate.

She moved against waves of freezing wind and pushed at leaden air, dragging her feet across the earth. She reeled and spun, striking at the force that tried to keep her. Sometimes crawling, sometimes walking backward or bent in half, she made her way through the garden, while ghostly glowing eyes marked her progress.

And then she was at the gate, where the vulture clung, his head twisted to glare at her with one stony eye. Dinah's courage almost failed her, but the shrill cry came again, demanding her to fight.

Closing her eyes against the sight of those dreadful talons, Dinah beat at the vulture with both fists. Her hands struck stone, but she heard the crackle of feathers as the hideous bird swung away.

Dinah flung herself through the open gate and toppled into the fresh air of the street.

The cat was crouching almost at her feet. It appeared even more wrecked and shabby than before. Dinah marveled that it had survived in such bitter weather. And then she was caught in the gaze of its green eyes and felt something of the cat's intrepid spirit.

This time they walked together, side by side, for she knew the cat was very weary. They both had the same destination. There was only a light powdering of snow in the street. Griffin's Castle had endured a private snowstorm.

The graveyard was silent. Peaceful. The cat crept into the small hollow beside Olwen Gwalchmai's headstone; it watched Dinah read again the words inscribed in the dark rock:

OLWEN, BELOVED WIFE OF TOMOS GWALCHMAI

She thought she might stay there all day. It was dry under the tree; its broad trunk and dense foliage were a shelter from the wind. It was Christmas Day. Someone would come, unlock the church door, and let her spend the night on a pew. She couldn't go back to Griffin's Castle alone.

A draft of frosty air sent her farther back under the branches. It was then that she became aware of the stranger standing behind her, so close to the tree that she had mistaken him for a shadow.

A host of horror stories raced through Dinah's mind. She had escaped from the stone creatures only to encounter the Angel of Death in a place she had thought would be safe. There was nowhere left to run, yet run she must.

The man, sensing her panic, said, "Don't be afraid, girl."

Dinah half turned, her throat dry with terror. She saw a very old man, dressed in a long tweed coat and a checked cap. His skin had the look of leather, tough and lined, and his dark eyes were hooded like those of a bird.

Dinah shrank from the stranger, wishing she could

find the words to send him away. But he moved closer and, nodding at the headstone, said, "I won't harm you, girl. I am here for my wife."

An astonished kind of joy swept over Dinah. She could recognize him now, beneath the wear of harsh mountain weather. She could see the young man and his wife, laughing at the sky while sheep moved behind them like white flowers.

Dinah found her voice. "Olwen Gwalchmai?"

"Olwen Gwalchmai." He smiled.

"She's my great-grandmother."

He peered at her for a long time. She couldn't tell if he didn't believe her or was trying to remember a name. "Dinah!" he said at last, and held out his hands.

As they walked back to Griffin's Castle together, Dinah's great-grandfather talked about his wife. He told Dinah all the things he'd been wanting to tell for such a long, long time. He talked about the seasons and the farm and his wild little ewes, about the room with a view of the mountain that had been waiting for someone to claim it: first a daughter, then a granddaughter. "But your mother was always moving on," he said, "and I could never find you."

And Dinah couldn't speak; she could only think of the room that was waiting and how it might look with a glass of wildflowers in the window.

Then her great-grandfather told her about the kitten with four white feet that he'd brought on one of his visits to Olwen's grave. "It was your first birthday," he told Dinah. "But I was dizzy with the noise of the city, and I fell, didn't I? Oh, nothing serious, but the kitten ran away. I didn't give up, mind. I would telephone your grandmother from the post office — I don't have a telephone, you understand — and she would give an address, but you had always gone from there."

"She never told us," Dinah said angrily.

"Some people like to cut out the past," he told her. "Make a fresh start. You can't blame them."

"I do," said Dinah, "because she did it without asking me. I've got a right to know where I belong."

"Well done, girl!" His laughter seemed to bring the deserted street to life.

They had reached Griffin's Castle. Tomos Gwalchmai frowned at the forlorn building in its shadowy garden.

"You can't stay there, Dinah," he said.

"But you will come in, won't you?" Dinah begged. "I've got a tree and decorations. It's still alive, you see. It was such a fine house."

"I can see you've got imagination!" He smiled. "I'll come and look at your decorations, but tomorrow I'm taking you back to Snowdonia, if you'll come. We'll be home for New Year's Day."

Dinah could hardly believe it. To cover her amazement and her happiness, she said, "There's some water in the kettle, so I can make you a cup of tea. And I've got tons of food. We can have a Christmas feast."

She had forgotten the animals. Were they still there, hiding in the trees, ready to pounce?

Before she could warn him, Tomos Gwalchmai had opened the gate and stepped inside, and Dinah thought she heard the faint chorus of wild animals and the swift patter of feet receding down the street. Although she was glad they were gone, she wasn't angry with them. They hadn't meant to harm her. They had just wanted to keep her with them.

As she followed her great-grandfather, Dinah dropped two small packages into the mailbox. "They're for my friends," she explained. "They said they might come. I haven't been very kind to them, but maybe they'll forgive me."

The cat watched her from the other side of the road. They had walked too fast for him, and he was resting for a moment before making a dash for the open gate.

A black car rolled up Anglesey Road. The driver was lost. He had spent the night in the city, but now he wanted to get home. He was scanning the walls for a road sign and didn't see the cat run across his path, but he felt something bump against a wheel. He sped away from whatever he had hit without looking into his mirror.

Dinah heard the soft thump and felt it like a blow. She tore into the street and, lifting up the scrawny cat, hugged him close.

"Oh, dear! Oh, dear! Oh, dear!" was all she could say.

Tomos Gwalchmai came and put his arms around her. Then he felt the cat's bones, very gently, lifting each limb. "He's not dead," he told her. "Look, his eyes are open. This old man is good with animals. We'll take him home and patch him up."

But Dinah couldn't stop sobbing. Now that she had remembered how to cry, she wept for all the years of suffering the old cat had endured. She clung to him, his scarred face against her cheek, while her great-grandfather led her into the house.

Jacob and Barry met at the top of Anglesey Road. It was almost dark. It had been a great day, but they were both glad to be out in the fresh air. Jacob had brought his present from Uncle Tadeusz; he drew the long curved sword out of a leather scabbard tied to his belt.

"Wow!" said Barry. "That's a beauty."

Jacob danced across the pavement, slicing the air with his sword. "It's not the real thing, of course," he said. "My uncle found it in a junk shop. He says it's pretty close, though."

"Did you bring Dinah's present?"

"Yes!"

"What shall we do if she's not there?"

"Put them in the box by the gate," Jacob said.

Griffin's Castle loomed in the dusk, a dark hulk whose shape could hardly be defined against the sky. There was a rectangle of soft light on the first floor, and the boys could see the little Christmas tree, adorned with stars, standing in the window. Beyond the tree they saw Dinah, sitting by a fire. She had managed to set the great mirror above the fireplace, and a row of candles placed before the shining glass filled the room with a warm sparkling light.

"It's funny," Barry remarked. "But it looks like Christmas *should* be in there, with candles an' all."

Impetuous Jacob sprang up to sit on the wall. Now he could see farther into the room. "She's got a visitor," he said.

Barry clambered up beside him. "Looks like Santa Claus," he remarked with a grin, for although the visitor wasn't dressed in scarlet, he did have a fine head of very white hair.

"And he's brought her a kitten," Jacob exclaimed. "I can see it on her lap."

"Safer than a lioness," said Barry, peering nervously at the trees.

But the animals had gone, leaving the garden mysteriously hollow, as though time had caught its breath for a moment before Griffin's Castle slipped into the past.

"Let's sing a carol." Jacob stood up, planting his feet wide on the bumpy surface of the wall.

Barry looked doubtful.

"Come on," Jacob insisted, and he began to sing in a funny tuneless voice. "Good King Wenceslas looked out, on the feast of Stephen!"

"Carol singers!" said Dinah's great-grandfather, and laughed. "Are they friends of yours?"

Still cradling the cat, Dinah walked over to the window and tried to make out where the voices came from. Two shadowy figures were balanced precariously on the distant wall. She knew who they were. The strange high voices that reached her across the empty garden were unmistakable. Soon they would look into the mailbox and find what she had left for them: the wooden bear for Jacob and the wolf for Barry. She had printed their names quite clearly, so there would be no confusion. "Yes, they're my friends," she said.

"Do you want to ask them in?"

She smiled and shook her head. "They don't really want to come in," she told him. "They just needed to know that I was safe. I'll send them a card from Snowdonia, shall I? A picture of our mountain."

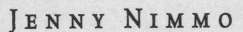

JENNY NIMMO

is an award-winning author who lives
with her painter husband in a converted
mill in Wales. She has written the
acclaimed Charlie Bone books, which
have repeatedly found their way onto
the *New York Times* and *USA Today*
bestseller lists; the Magician's Trilogy,
including *The Snow Spider*, winner of
the Smarties Prize, *Emyln's Moon*, and
The Chestnut Soldier; and *The Owl Tree*,
which won the Smarties Gold Prize
Award. *Griffin's Castle* was short-listed
for the Smarties Prize, the Carnegie
Medal, and the Whitbread Award.